THE STORY OF ZAHRA

Also by
Hanan al-Shaykh

Women of Sand and Myrrh

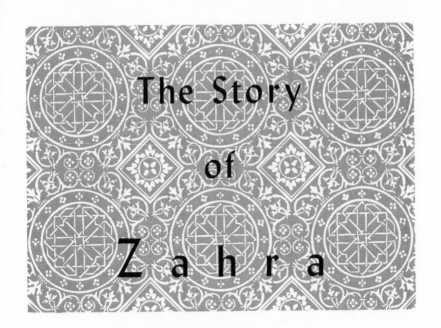

The Story of Zahra

HANAN AL-SHAYKH

ANCHOR BOOKS

DOUBLEDAY

NEW YORK LONDON TORONTO SYDNEY AUCKLAND

AN ANCHOR BOOK
PUBLISHED BY DOUBLEDAY
a division of Bantam Doubleday Dell Publishing Group, Inc.
1540 Broadway, New York, New York 10036

ANCHOR BOOKS, DOUBLEDAY, and the portrayal of an anchor
are trademarks of Doubleday, a division of Bantam Doubleday
Dell Publishing Group, Inc.

Book design by Terry Karydes

First published in English by Quartet Books Limited U.K. in 1986.

The Anchor Books edition is published by
arrangement with Quartet Books Limited.

The text of *The Story of Zahra* was rendered into English by
Peter Ford with the author's cooperation.

Library of Congress Cataloging-in-Publication Data
Shaykh, Ḥanān.
[Ḥikāyat Zahrah. English]
The story of Zahra / Hanan al-Shaykh;
[rendered into English by Peter Ford with the author's co-operation].
— 1st Anchor Books ed.
p.   cm.
I. Title.
PJ7862.H356H5513   1994
892'.736—dc20   93-3678
CIP

ISBN 0-385-47130-0

Contents

Glossary

Ahlan wa sahlan: Welcoming greeting.

Bourj: Open central square in downtown Beirut.

Classical Arabic: Written Arabic not usually spoken except on formal occasions.

Coup d'état: In 1949 the PPS attempted an unsuccessful *coup d'état* after which its leader Antoun Saadeh was executed.

Fertile Crescent: The area encompassing Syria, Lebanon, Jordan and Palestine/Israel.

Firaké: A variant of *kibbé* special to the Shi'a community in Southern Lebanon.

Foul: A dish of dried beans eaten with olive oil and lemon.

Gazouza: Fizzy drink.

Greater Syria: A geographical term used to describe the lands of the Fertile Crescent.

Karantina: Refugee camp from after the 1918 War.

Kibbé: Dish made of ground meat and cracked wheat.

Kishk: Dried yogurt.

Melokhia: Ancient Egyptian soup-like dish made of a green leaf of the mallow family.

Muaidi: A poet and man of letters renowned for his ugliness.

PPS: Popular Syrian Party founded by Antoun Saadeh advocating a Greater Syrian state.

"Red Storm": A swastika within a circle, emblem of the PPS.

Shawarma: Layers of closely packed meat cooked on a revolving spit.

Book One

The Scars of Peace

1

Zahra Remembers

We stood trembling behind the door. I was aware that my heartbeats mingled with the pulse in her hand as it stayed firmly pressed to my mouth. Her hand smelled of soap and onions. I wished she would keep it there for ever. The hand was plump and warm. We hid in the darkness behind the door slightly ajar. Sounds of footsteps and loud noises drew nearer, before the door fully opened and light streamed into the room. Instinctively we glued ourselves to the wall behind the door and a current of fear ran through us as if we were wired together.

Now, as her fingers squeezed my mouth, I realized that my heartbeats had melted away and her pulse had died down from the extent of our fear. Only as a huge fat head peered into the room, seeing yet not seeing us, only then did I fathom the reason for that fear, and the reason for her hand tightly cupping my mouth. Yet what I attempted to understand was, at best, blurred. My mother had, as usual, made me wear my navy woollen trousers and knitted green top. She had plaited my hair while, every now and then, dipping the comb into a glass of water. As she worked she had warned me, in a voice loud enough for my father to overhear, that she would spank me if I disobeyed her in the way I usually did whenever she took me to Dr. Shawky's. As her voice went on, I tried to remember whether Dr. Shawky had given me an injection, and couldn't somehow recall that he had. She held my hand as we went down the stairs and I was still trying hard to remember. I asked my mother: "Why does he want to give me an injection? Is it because I am lazy in school? Or because the teacher said she would rub my face with yogurt and shut me in the 'rat room' for always wetting my pants in class?" She replied: "Oh! Keep quiet! Isn't it enough that I have sold my gold bracelets to buy you your calcium injections? Don't you see how bow-legged you are?" And then she added, looking at my feet: "One points to the left, the other to the right."

So we hid behind the door. The tears at the back of my eyes somehow lost their way while trying to spill out. We were both still standing, her white hand this time squeezing my hand instead of my mouth, when a white face appeared in the doorway and peered into the darkness, seeing yet not seeing us. Her hand relaxed only when the face disappeared and the door again closed.

In spite of our clinging bodies, I felt cold and frightened. After a while—how long it was I couldn't judge—not fully understanding what had already happened and what was about to happen, I only knew that I felt cold and frightened.

Again the door opened and closed, and I heard a key turn in the lock. Then I saw a face I knew: the face of a man I had seen before, leaning his head on my mother's lap; a man the colors and patterns of whose suit are for ever registered in my mind. He had once visited us at home, accompanied by a woman. He was the same man who, whenever I saw him, would reach into his pocket and bring out a pink rubber doll for me to play with and then would lift me up. Now he was standing facing us, holding my mother's hand, my mother holding my hand, the three of us sitting on the bed. Or was I not sitting? Perhaps I was leaning against my mother's thigh. I continued to feel shivery and uncomfortable, though the fear eventually vanished. Even so, I knew quite well by now that we had not gone to Dr. Shawky's as my mother had said, and as she had assured me, and as I had continued to believe, in spite of the garden walls we had passed not being those we usually saw on our way to Dr. Shawky's. These had not had black splotches on them. I knew the story of those other walls, and the story of the bat which each night attacked the mulberry tree owned by "Mulberry" Muhammad; which spotted the wall opposite with crimson and dark blue blotches. I always wondered why the bat splattered the mulberries rather than ate them. Why did he choose this mulberry tree? On that day I had not seen the mulberry tree or looked for the bat, or even asked if the bat plucked out people's eyes!

The route we were taking to Dr. Shawky's house was the best one, my mother assured me, and I believed her. I had to continue believing her, even though everything pointed to the contrary: there was no sign of Dr. Shawky, the atmosphere of the visit was different, and no needle had been jabbed into my thigh that morning. In vain do I try to remember the details of that morning in that room which was not Dr. Shawky's. In vain do I try to remember the words exchanged between this man and my mother. Perhaps it is because I was so young, or perhaps such an accumulation of days has followed this visit that the distant past has been

obscured. Or perhaps because I had anticipated the visit to
Dr. Shawky, my mind had conjured up an image of the
surgery, the furniture in it and the doctor's familiar face. All
of those details have become stuck irrevocably in my mind
to the extent where they overlay much else.

But I do remember our arrival in Damascus, my mother,
me, and her friend, whom I never liked and who sensed the
hatred I felt for her as well. I hated her dark complexion,
and the fullness of her lips, her wavy thick braids. At times,
on the journey, she would express her own dislike of me
with harsh, piercing stares. At other times, when the man
stopped the car at my mother's behest, after I had warned
her, by whispering in her ear, that I was going to throw up,
she would say, "How painfully tiresome you are, girl.
You're the absolute limit!" The moment I left the car, the
nausea ceased, and guilt set in as I got into the car once
more. Then I would catch that look in my mother's friend's
eye: a look filled with disgust and impatience as the car
stopped a second and then a third and a fourth time, until
my mother refused to listen to me and her friend resumed
smoking and chewing gum. At that point I lost all control
and finally vomited down my front, then all over my
mother, who withdrew her left hand from the driver's thigh
as their voices grew louder and louder.

Ever since the day before I had kept telling myself, "I am
on my way to Damascus." When we were finally in Damascus I said, "I am in Damascus, and only a while ago I was
somewhere else." Yet it really made no difference, except
that the tiny room in which my mother made me lie down
had new tiles and furniture. I wanted to stay awake, but
sleep and heat overcame me. When I heard a knocking on
the door, I couldn't open my eyes at first. I was so tired.
The knocking grew louder and a voice kept shouting,

"Open the door. This is a hotel, not a brothel!" It was then that I jumped to my feet. I saw my mother rise from the sheets and the man turn his face and body away from me as he pulled on his trousers. I was suddenly surprised to see the man and my mother in the same bed. Was it because I had grown a little and could understand certain things better? Or was it because I knew that my mother and father always slept in separate beds? The knocking and voices at the door had ceased. When my mother opened the door, the angry man who had been knocking saw me standing, clinging to her.

Here is another memory. I am at an age when I can fully distinguish between village and city life. I am afraid of eye infections, so will not eat figs or even go near a fig tree since I have been told that figs make the eyes go sore. I wash my hands in a tin pitcher which I hold firmly between my thighs, and bend over, trying to keep the pitcher balanced so that the water pours out smoothly without spilling in a rush as it did the first time I visited the village. The village means eggs fried over burning thorns, mosquito bites on my face and body, and Mustapha humming at the straw booth's door, "*Dumanu . . . Dumdudu.*" I am not going to eat a fig, will not touch one, nor even touch my eyes when walking between the fig trees. I will cover my eyes with my hand and ask Mustapha to take me back to the straw booth where my mother is. He asks me who told me that figs redden the eyes and I answer: "I heard our neighbor in Beirut say so when we were getting ready to come to the village." ("You are going to pick figs and get red eyes.") Mustapha laughs and laughs and refuses to return to the straw booth until the tears begin to roll down my face. Then his humming grows louder and turns into a song as we draw closer to the straw booth: "We are a-coming, a-coming, a-coming. We have come, we have come-come-come. And we have brought the bride with us!"

My mother, in her blue patterned dress, her hair swept up by a comb, looks out from inside the tent. The man looks over her shoulder, the man who kisses and holds me and gives me a small doll to play with. He looks out, holding a white handkerchief over his nose and bringing his chin close to his neck and pulling at his nostrils. Then he throws his head backwards, spreads open the handkerchief and, once again, covers his nose and blows it. My mother anxiously tries to say something. "How did that wretched mosquito get in here?" Mustapha says nothing. He knows that a gnat must have flown up the man's nose.

I suddenly feel as if the village has slipped away from my grasp and that my mother is no longer present. This man has followed us here, where previously it was only my mother, the wind and me. The distance between me and my mother grows greater, deeper, although we have been as close as an orange and its navel. That closeness, these lingering days when the sun leaps high over our heads and sets as we make our way homeward . . . all that time enables me to study my mother closely.

I would watch her when she was with me, and study her when she was at a distance. I thought all the while, as I looked up at her, of how much I wanted to draw her towards me, to draw myself close to her, to touch her face and have her eyes peering into mine. I wanted to disappear into the hem of her dress and become even closer to her than the navel is to the orange!

But whenever I began to think in this way, I felt a bitterness towards her and shuddered. I carried this pain and hatred inside me whenever I disobeyed her and felt rejected, neglected by her. The man became the center of her life, and around him was nothing but flying embers. I would question myself incessantly, yet the nameless feeling persisted. Even today I still ask myself what was the nature of this feeling. Was it jealousy? Was it pity for my father? Or was it the fear that took hold of me every time I accompanied her on one of her assignations with the man? These encounters made my view of things blurred, as if seen through rain-splattered glass or steamed-up mirrors. My thoughts were unclear and seemed to relate to nothing in particular. They could arrive at no conclusions.

I remember her sitting under a green walnut tree with his head in her lap as she sang to his closed eyes, "Oh, my sleeping love." He, whose face and hair were so opaque. He, whose body was sprawled and relaxed under the burnished mountain rocks, reddened, dustless, sandless. The inviting stones were as clean as if someone had poured a stream of water over them, then dyed them with the sun's rays and the shade of the walnut tree. Whenever I saw the man and my mother together and heard her voice, I would squat like an old woman and cry out so loud that the whole world and even outer space might have heard me. But they did not. My mother still sang on. Her voice still murmured, "Oh, my sleeping love." And always I was ignored. I would start crying and watch the scene re-enacted over and over: her hand stroking his hair as she hummed, "Oh, my sleeping love."

Their secrets lost some of their mystery as I grew older and began regretfully to look back. Now I resented her all the more for having immersed me in a well of doubts and questions and magic while still so young and vulnerable. Only today do I fully know why we stood trembling behind that door and what that man's large head, peering in, seeing yet not seeing us, meant. And the splattered wall where the bats landed, "Mulberry" Muhammad's tree, Damascus, my nausea, the single bed. Only now do I understand the mystery of our walking through the rain as the mud sucked our feet down and the trees seemed like human beings with watchful eyes; our running, then stopping, my mother greeting someone and suddenly pulling me away before I could recognize who it was, sighing a big sigh as we continued to run in the rain and splash through the mud.

As for my father, he was preoccupied with the tramway. It would not have surprised me if he had come home one day pulling his tram-car behind him. His watch, which he kept in the pocket of his khaki trousers, hung on a chain. Each night his fingers would set the alarm, and each morning his hand would reach out to quiet its ringing. He would pull on his trousers, check the watch was working by bringing it close to his ear, then slip it back into his pocket. He would put on his khaki shirt, reach for his hat, and become totally monochrome in khaki. He would say, "Zahra, don't be late for school, and you, Ahmad, don't forget to bring home your school tuition receipt." His working day on the tram ran from early morning to evening. He would announce his return home by pulling the rope attached to a small bell in the corner of our living room. He always insisted on ringing this bell before entering his own house. "How are you, and where is Ahmad?" He would hang up his cap. "Where is your mother?" he would ask, taking off his khaki jacket and hanging it on a chair. He never omitted to reach into his pocket, bring out his watch, listen to its ticking and return it to its place. "Where's Ahmad?"

We would sit around our kitchen table as Ahmad and I watched our father eat *melokhia,* rich in chicken meat, or was it cloves of garlic? I dared not reach for the chicken pieces since I had been given dinner earlier, my meal also consisting of *melokhia*, but without any chicken meat. Every evening it was the same. My mother would never give me a single morsel of meat. This she always reserved for Ahmad, sometimes for my father. Her ways never changed. Maybe she never ate chicken or meat herself. I am sure she never did at our earlier meal together. Every day, as we sat in the kitchen to eat, her love would be declared: having filled my plate with soup she serves my brother Ahmad, taking all her time, searching carefully for the best pieces of meat. She dips the ladle into the pot and salvages meat fragments. There they go into Ahmad's dish. There they sit in Ahmad's belly.

My mother intervenes to break a silence, saying, "To-morrow I want to take Zahra along with me to the village. My father's ill. Mustapha phoned the store-keeper and said so. Let me have five liras."

My father frowns, he remains silent, does not give her the five liras. Nevertheless she takes them from his jacket while he is still in the kitchen. I tell her to be careful, that he can see her. All she does is smile when I point to the picture hanging on the wall. It is a portrait of him in his khaki uniform.

The next day we visited my healthy, red-cheeked grand-father, who threaded tobacco leaves on to skewers to dry as quickly and expertly as if he were rolling his moustache. The same man would join us at the village, but not at my grandfather's, who would think my mother had come to pick up a document from the registry. She refused to re-main longer than half an hour with my grandfather in the booth hung with green tobacco leaves, and all the time I wanted to throw myself into the old man's arms and beg him to let me stay with him in the warm, protecting booth. It was hard for me to face those feelings which I dreaded but couldn't explain—that mixture of shyness, jealousy and fear among other things. Would they choose an apple or an orange tree, or another kind of tree to lie under this time?

The car stopped by the beach. I could only see a withered tree, and garbage strewn on the white sands. I picked up the broken high heel of an old shoe, and how they laughed and winked at each other when they saw it in my hand. And how I hated them at that moment! They embarrassed me, made me feel unsure of myself, alone.

What then? The surroundings were new to me. We did not go close to the tree or the sea. Instead we entered a little house which contained almost no furniture. The man left us there as he went to fetch a package from the car and my mother and I exchanged questioning looks. Why did she always have to take me along? Did she have any idea of how I suffered? Perhaps not. I never protested. The man interrupted my thoughts. After fiddling with the package, he tore the broiled chicken it contained apart with his hands and served it up on plates made of paper—something I had never before seen. I held my extraordinary piece of chicken and I thought to myself that, if my grandfather were to ask me if I had enjoyed it, I would answer, "No, no, grandfather." I felt so embarrassed in the presence of this man, worried that I might make noises chewing and swallowing. Too embarrassed to lift my hand to my mouth and spit into it a small bone, I preferred to swallow the bone and suffer the hurt in my throat. I was too embarrassed also to eat the meat close to the bone, despite its tantalizing smell and my hunger. "No, dear grandfather, I did not enjoy it at all."

Once we had done eating, a discussion followed which made me realize why it was that my mother always took me along. She actually needed my protection. She wanted us to be inseparable, like the "orange and navel." She wanted me to shield her. Their discussion concerned whether I should go out to play in the sand, but her answer was an immediate, "No," although both she and I knew that I would never open my mouth and say what was in my soul. Then she quickly told of a dream she had had the night before in which she was tearing at her hair in grief, and said how she would worry so if I ever went near the water. He again asked whether Zahra would like to sit on the stairs to play with a pretty doll, which he then produced. It was always the same rubber doll. I remained as still as a statue. My mother said she feared the devil would whisper to me and drag me towards the sea. The man then asked her to go with him into the other room, where he wanted to show her something. She stood to follow him, and we looked at each other, my eyes pleading for her to stay. I wanted to pull her close to me, but would hear the door close and be left alone with my tears. I wished I could push open that door . . .

It was a feeling which shattered both reality and imagination. It was much as I felt when I rode the roller-coaster with Ibtisam. The ride was so high and so fast, racing between heaven and earth. It suspended me between sky and land like a bolt of lightning, and when we touched the ground again I felt as if my legs were dropping off and rolling away from under me. The roller-coaster would go up and down, round and about. My body would stiffen, my heart pound as I clutched the iron bars which grew slippery with perspiration as my teeth chattered and I cursed this game and myself for going through with the horrible experience. As it went hurtling down I would think that it must be like a descent into hell, plunging into nothingness.

Thus I wished I might open the door, although I didn't quite know what I would see behind it, other than his head in her lap, her hand feeding him, or his arms about her, as when, under the walnut tree, he lifted her with one shoe falling off and called her "Mama." I only knew that between this man and my mother there were shared secrets.

The blows fell on my face and head. I tried to think clearly as the words of the Lord of the Tram-car thundered and drowned out the nervous voice of my mother, afraid I might reveal all: "Tell the truth! Where did you used to go with your mother? Where did he used to take the two of you?"

My mother cried out, "By God, you are mad, Ibrahim! Leave the child alone. Everything you hear is lies and slander! Leave the girl alone, Ibrahim!"

He paid no attention to her, but continued to shower me with blows, his voice lashing at me, the words torn out from between his lips. I knew only dread of this god in his khaki suit, dread of his tram-car, dread of his strong body—that particular dread the strongest of all. I shook all over as I burst into a sobbing that couldn't drown out my mother's screams. He slapped her face and seized her hair. She ran into the kitchen, leaving me trapped in the room, like a wooden post, choking out an occasional sob. I heard my father shout, "You must be insane, Fatmé! Shame on you! You must be out of your mind!" while she whimpered, "Leave me be. I wish to die."

I don't recall how I entered the kitchen and smelled the petroleum, saw her pressed against the cupboard, squirming in his grip as she tried to free herself, wailing, "Leave me be! I wish to die." I wanted then to run to her, to pull her to me so we could again become like orange and navel, and began to cry and whimper with her. I no longer knew where I stood, what my feelings were, to whom I owed my loyalty. All I knew was that I was afraid of my father, as afraid of the blows he dealt her as I was of those he dealt me; while she continued to tremble and wail in his grip. I heard her say, in the midst of her self-deceptions, "I swear by God, by the holy shrine of Kaaba, that I didn't take off a stocking in his presence. He only gave me a ride once from Riad al-Solh, because it was raining. I swear by Sitt Zaynab, the daughter of the Prophet, I never took off my stockings." My father calmed down a little as he heard the last sentence, but after a few moments he began to shout like a madman, "Fatmé, do you swear by the Qur'an?" She answered, wailing, "I'd swear a thousand times. I swear by the Qur'an. I swear by the shrine of Sitt Zaynab."

As he let her go, I ran back to my own room. I tried to wipe away the traces of my embarrassment from the floor and thought of stockings. Then I heard more crying and moaning, and muffled angry voices. I wondered why the wailing had started again. Frightened and sobbing, I burst out of my room and went back into the kitchen.

My mother was sprawled on the kitchen floor as my father, in his khaki suit, his leather belt in one hand, was beating her. In the other hand he held a Qur'an as he demanded, "Swear! Swear! Show me!" She pressed her face against the floor tiles as he repeated like a drugged man, "Swear!" Sometimes adding, "Prove it to me."

Seeing the blood covering her face, I tore at my hair and beat my chest, exactly as she would do herself. Then I stood on a chair and, reaching for the window, pushed aside the still-fresh orange peels laid there to dry. I meant to cry for help to our neighbor Issa, but my father, thinking I was about to jump out the window, let my mother go and threw himself at me. At that moment, I really did want to jump for fear of him, while my mother gathered her strength and escaped to the bathroom, where she locked herself in.

2

Zahra in Africa

I thought I would recognize my Uncle Hashem's face the moment my feet touched the ground at that African airport, despite having seen him no more than five times in all my life. He rarely visited us "before running away to Africa," to live as an exile, yet he remained a presence among us wherever he happened to be, however he happened to fare.

He was always mentioned in family conversations, even before he fled from Lebanon. He was always on my grandfather's mind and in my aunt's heart. My Aunt Wafaa was only two years older than me, so that we used to forget we were aunt and niece in our friendship. Everything which had to do with my uncle, however, was out of the ordinary: his conversation, his life style, his food, his friends. He even left home and lived from time to time in a rented room in a block close to the American University.

I would hear Wafaa tell my grandfather, whenever we visited him in the south, that Hashem would eat oysters and other shell-fish, that he had bought a record player and records and tried to teach Wafaa and her friends to tango. During the summer, he lived in an elegant hotel in Dhour Al-Shuwair where he used to swim. He would park his rented motor-bike in front of police headquarters, defying the janitor's threats. He would invite girls over to his parents' town house while they were away in the village, ignoring the scandalized eyes of neighbors. He would wear Cologne as he walked down the street whistling, his hands in his pockets, strutting, showing off his athletic shoulders. He also used to hold political meetings in his parents' house. He was a member of the PPS, the Lebanese party which works for a "Greater Syria," and had drawn its emblem, the "Red Storm," on the house walls.

He could be cruel to his sister Wafaa. My grandfather's constant comment was, "Is there anyone in the world who can stand up to Hashem?" But my grandfather would add, while in his shed threading tobacco leaves, "Hashem is so forceful that, if he hadn't been in Beirut, I would have brought his mother and Wafaa back to live in the village long before."

My uncle's face was imprinted on my mind from the many pictures of him which hung in the living rooms of all our relatives' homes. Those pictures were recorded in my memory down to the most minute detail, because in some of them were naked Africans . . . naked except for their necklaces of beads and ivory.

While I was looking about for him at the airport, he recognized me by a simple process of elimination. He said later, "You were the only young girl. The others were all women."

I thought: "Women, breasts, gold bracelets, and children in their bellies. Children hanging on their arms. Milk bottles, and dummies in their handbags."

He came nearer and greeted me with a kiss on the cheek. I quickly kissed him back, then he embraced me with all his strength, both arms around me. I felt uncomfortable, but urged myself to relax and think, "This is how I used to embrace my grandfather. My uncle is, after all, his son."

He sighed and said, "For the first time I have a feeling of being back home."

I saw how different he was from his pictures and my own faded memory. How much shorter and plumper he was.

When he spoke, I recognized that he was my uncle. His tone of voice and southern accent were like my mother's. So was the color and texture of his hair. But I felt uncomfortable and uneasy with him in the car, suddenly regretting having accepted his invitation. Embarrassment perhaps best expressed my feeling. I thought, I will remain here only a month, instead of the few months or year which I originally planned. A whole month? What shall we talk about? How will I react? I tried to avoid these thoughts by asking about another aunt who lived in a neighboring town. When we arrived at his house, there was a message from his servant, informing him that he would be late for dinner. I asked if his servant slept in the house. He said no. I suddenly felt upset.

I entered his room, now to be mine, and liked it. It was modest, and there were shelves of books in Arabic and a typical Lebanese calendar on the wall.

When my uncle came into the room, he sat down, facing me, and began to talk about Lebanon, about Zionist propaganda here and of how Lebanon made no attempt to counter Zionist lies. He spoke of our homeland, and I saw how very idealistic he was about his country. At first, I discussed nothing with him, I paid no attention to his words, but he repeated the same things over and over until I real-

ized how deeply he wished to return home. Here, in Africa,
he carried in his mind a symbolic image of his homeland,
believing this to be the actual homeland, the every-day
homeland. Here, among thousands of blacks in Africa, he
saw himself as lording it over them and wondered why he
couldn't be back in his own country. He thought constantly
of his country, its mountains and valleys, the sea there.
Again and again his conversation returned to the same
point. He remembered his homeland with remarkable viv-
idness.

His idealism was so intense. When I could take no more
of it I would cry out, "Please! Let me get to the bathroom."
All I had to do was push open a kitchen door and go along
a narrow corridor, filled with TV sets, radios and records,
stacked on shelves to the ceiling. When I saw these for the
first time, I was afraid they might tumble on my head. The
second time I felt safer. The third time, I looked up to make
sure they were all still in place. I would relax once I was in
the small bathroom at the end of the corridor, and plan
what I would do during the day; and would, before long, be
using that as a bolt-hole.

My uncle soon began to pester me. Every morning at
seven he would come into my room and move about in it
while I pretended to stay asleep until he gave up. He would
draw open the curtains, but I would remain rigid, motionless. Then he would move to the living room and turn up
the radio very loud. I would keep my eyes shut . . . stay
silent. Next he would come back to sit on my bed and
touch my face. At first I thought this must be quite a usual
way to wake someone up, although his hand would linger
on my cheek until I drew away in embarrassment. Finally,
he would open the windows. This was the signal for me to
jump out of bed and ask to go to the bathroom. At first, I

couldn't understand why he wouldn't let me sleep as long as
I wanted. As I soon discovered, what he really wanted was
to attract my full attention.

His behavior troubled me to painful extremes, especially
one evening in the movies. As the film began, I was aware
of something which my mind at once rejected. I couldn't
somehow make it out or explain it. He had put an arm
round my shoulders and was hugging me. I was left breathless, incredulous, motionless as his hand squeezed my shoulder. I shifted and drew away, losing track of the film on the
screen. I couldn't follow anything at all. Suddenly it was as
if I was back in the small room in Damascus, waking up as
my mother jumped from under the bedsheets like a madwoman.

Then, just as vividly, I was at my aunt's in the area of the
Hotel Dieu hospital, with my grandfather, after he had carried a metal container of fresh milk from the south all the
way to Beirut, only to drop it on my aunt's doorstep. He
made me sit on his lap, as if he was trying to forget this
minor disaster. As I sat there I felt safe, my hand on his
back. I loved my grandfather, loved him for the love he
showed me. I sat happily on his knee, watching my aunt
busily occupied with collecting up the laundry which she
had earlier spread out to dry on some bushes. She plucked
some small dry leaves and held them for my grandfather to
smell.

He cried out, cheering up, "Ah! This green tea has a
scent like baklava!" Then he asked my aunt if he could have
a cigarette. As she went back towards the bushes, I whispered in my grandfather's ear, asking whether she would
now pluck him a cigarette from among the leaves. He
laughed, "No, no, Zahra!"

Jumping off his lap, I followed my aunt into the kitchen.

She opened the kitchen cupboard and handed me two cigarettes. I realized I was in a different world. My aunt's window overlooked a hospital ward. I could see nurses clad in white and a bar of soap on a window sill as my nose was filled with hospital odors.

That night we stayed with my aunt, who was getting ready to go to Africa within the next few days. She was leaving behind her son Kasem to enroll at the university in Beirut. When my grandfather asked about Kasem, she replied, "He'll be here shortly." When Kasem arrived in due course, he bent to kiss my grandfather's hand and looked at me closely as if struggling to think who I was. My aunt noticed his look and laughingly said, "Come, come, Kasem, don't you recognize your cousin Zahra, the daughter of my sister Fatmé?"

Embarrassed, Kasem stammered, "But of course I remember her! How's Ahmad these days? Which school does he go to?"

My grandfather then voiced his disappointment: "This family acts like strangers. No visits between its members. They behave more like enemies. They are a family in name only!" Later, as I was sleeping on the floor next to my grandfather, in a darkness so intense as to be completely saturated with darkness, it seemed as if a cold hand furtively moved in my panties. I woke and jumped up in a fright, and the hand suddenly disappeared. But the fear and the coldness had gripped me and shaken me. Even in that total darkness that could absorb no more darkness, I thought, for an instant, I saw the glint of Kasem's spectacles. Then there was nothing. It was an uneasy night, an unreal night. I stayed awake till dawn. I did not relax my head on the pillow until a faint light began to fill the room.

After that, my aunt's footsteps approached our mattress.

"Come on, father, wake up, say your prayers. It is almost 5:30, nearly time for your dawn prayers." My grandfather woke mumbling. I remembered the night before and my sleeplessness, and felt full of melancholy and apprehension.

It was the same feeling which came over me later in the movie theater. There it canceled out all the regard I felt for my uncle. His fingers searched for and held my hand, and I gathered courage to withdraw it and shake him off. My clasped hands prayed he would not try again. My own fingers intertwined and I bled beads of sweat. I wished that instead they could be beads of blood. My face, all of me, would be bleeding then. If only I could bleed without having to suffer wounds.

I bled like a fountain, felt like crying, like running away, like screaming until the movie finished and the lights came up. Hatred for the darkness, for the faces of the audience which gaped at the screen, welled up in me. Then I thought how the lights would soon flood the auditorium and everyone leave; uncle and I drive back to his house. I wished then that the movie might never end; or that, after the lights came up, many days and nights might pass in safety to give me a chance of burying my sadness and unease. Yet I knew I could never forget. Sitting in the car, I could not bring myself to broach the subject, but wished I could simply say, "Please don't ruin my visit. You're upsetting me."

The days passed. I tried to bury my wounds, but kept thinking of my uncle's hand squeezing my shoulders, my uncle behaving towards me like a man to a woman.

The sense of sadness completely enfolded me. I retreated into my shell. What choice did I have? The hand had been my uncle's hand. Supposing I had screamed? How could we have looked each other in the eye afterwards? How could I have gone back with him to his house? If I had decided to

return to Beirut there and then, how could I have let him
see me off at the airport? And now it could only look as
though I had encouraged him. After all, I hadn't repulsed
his hand or protested. Instead, each morning, I merely
locked the bathroom door and stayed a prisoner, even as I
used to seek refuge in the bathroom back home in Beirut
when I was afraid of my father's penetrating eyes—afraid he
would discover what I had grown into, afraid he would kill
me. My father was always brutal. His appearance seemed to
express his character: a frowning face, a Hitler-like moustache above thick full lips, a heavy body. Do I misjudge
him? He had a stubborn personality. He saw all life in terms
of black or white.

Perhaps his harsh character saved me from disfiguring my
face more badly then I might otherwise have done. He
would scold me severely whenever he caught me playing
with my pimples. My fingers would search one out, touch
it, peel off the dry skin, then squeeze it out of existence. I
would not stop until I found a drop of blood on my finger.
It was as if my fingers had to go to work before I could say a
word. Even when I was about to respond to some question,
my fingers would begin probing. I would look at my face in
the mirror and see the widely distributed pimples with the
dried blood on them forming black and brown scabs. Then
I would write to some women's magazine and appeal for a
cure. My pimples were my only reason for waking each
morning. I would hurry to the mirror to inspect in the calm
light of day the ravages of the latest onslaught.

It was a long-standing habit. My father would go raving
mad every time he noticed my face and its problems. He
would nag my mother sarcastically: "That will be the day,
when Zahra marries. What a day of joy for her and her

pock-marked face!" Once he beat me when he caught me standing in front of the mirror, squeezing at my incipient spots.

Everyone I knew explained away the pimples in much the same way. "It's acne. It will soon disappear." Or they would say, "That's what you get for eating sweets." Or else, "It's because you eat pickles and hot peppers." But then my father would chip in, "It is because she is reckless. It is the work of her own hand." It used to disturb me greatly when he made such remarks.

My father's one dream was to save enough money to send my brother Ahmad to the United States to study electrical engineering. Why electrical engineering? I could not imagine. Ahmad could barely read and write. He was always being thrown out of school. Neither my father's harshness nor his threats ever had any effect on Ahmad. Yet my father's plan to send him to the States remained unshakable. Meat continued to be for Ahmad. Eggs were for Ahmad. Fresh tomatoes were for Ahmad. So were the fattest olives. If Ahmad was late arriving home, my mother would rumple his bed and push a pillow down under the bedclothes. If my father asked, she would mumble, "Ahmad is sleeping." She lied for her son, even when he tried to steal her gold bracelets as she slept. She once awoke in a panic to find a bangle dangling from her arm as Ahmad ran away. She went back to sleep after having refastened the gold bracelet on her arm.

Ahmad was seven years older than me. Between us there had been a set of twins, girl and boy, who lived but briefly in a porcelain soup dish after my mother aborted them. Why did she let those bodies no bigger than a finger swim in a soup dish while she lay sprawled on the bed? The offi-

cial midwife, Izdihar, shook her head, feeling sorry or
happy, I did not know which. There was no accounting for
it.

I remember the neighbors pouring into the bedroom to
greet my mother, then peering into the soup dish where the
tiny embryos swam. And then exclaiming, "In the name of
Allah, the All Merciful. Blessed be the Creator. Look, here
is a fully developed creature." But one was more forthright
and asked, "Why abortion after abortion?" Another grew
more outspoken still, and spat, swearing and shoving the
dish aside: "I spit on the human being. Is this how we all are
created—as minute as a finger nail becoming as huge as
mules!"

My mother would lean on a neighbor to visit the bathroom. Then she would return to bed, pale, yet with happiness almost jumping from her glistening eyes.

She didn't want to have children by my father. She would
mention the word "divorce" every time we visited grandfather in his tobacco booth, and always he would reproach
her, "For repentance, Fatmé. Acknowledge God. Repent,
my daughter!"

The feelings of disgust and fear that I felt for my uncle
made me wary about everything and constantly watching to
avoid any embarrassing situation. And then I once caught
him reading in my diary something I had written there the
night before. I found myself pouncing on him like a young
tigress. It wasn't strength that sustained me, but a guilty
conscience and embarrassment at what I had actually written:

As the proverb says, it's better to listen to the poet
Muaidi than it is to see him . . . I feel very disappointed now that I have seen my uncle. He sounded so

different in his letters. I'm afraid he's a very mixed-up person.

I snatched the diary from his hands. Evidently he had not yet read all of it, because he blustered nervously, "Why the anxiety? What is there to be afraid of? Why do you act like this?"

I sat, exhausted, on the bed. I thought his behavior as bad as my father's, especially when he angrily left the room. I went into the bathroom and heard myself thinking, "There is no parting from you, bathroom. You are the only thing I have loved in Africa. You, and the electrical appliances stacked on the shelves." I tore the scribbled page from my diary into tiny scraps and, because I could not trust my uncle, instead of flushing them down the toilet wrapped them in a piece of toilet paper and hid them in my underpants. Secure between my thighs, no one could even know what was written on them about my uncle. Then I sat and wrote on another page . . . my impressions of Africa, of the weather. Before I unlocked that bathroom door I was filled with a sense of happiness and congratulated myself on my cleverness and the sort of deception to which I always resorted when outwitting my father.

Stealthily I returned the diary to its former place on the bed, and when my uncle saw it back there, he picked it up, saying, "It makes a change to find you showing some sense." But as he prepared to read it, he added, "This has been newly written. You are a liar." And he resumed his frenzied search of the room, thrashing about as if he were an eagle which had mistakenly blundered in and was looking for a way out, or as if he were a hungry rat, scavenging for food. He went to the bathroom next and I heard the toilet flush, the water flow. Even though I could feel the scraps of

paper nestling below my belly, I was still afraid that he
might think of searching me. I wasn't even aware when he
stealthily slipped back into my room, hoping to catch me
hiding the papers. Those papers are secure between my
thighs, obstinate man! They are safe! Even if you were to
summon the best witch-doctor in Africa, he never would
trace them, unless those papers themselves called out and
betrayed me!

A night went past, my uncle scarcely speaking to me.
Next day his bachelor friends paid a visit and asked us out to
dinner. Once again I felt safe, as safe as I did in the narrow
bathroom at home in Beirut. I felt safe and at ease, although
I am not usually the slightest bit comfortable in the company of strangers. My hand automatically rises to touch the
acne on my face . . . On this occasion, though, I was
happy to see my uncle's friends.

In the restaurant to which we went out together there
was an African singer who sang, with much depth of feeling, in both French and Spanish. One of my uncle's friends,
Majed, invited me to dance, but I became covered in confusion. I had only ever danced once before, at a school func-
tion with a younger girl. I danced without any rhythm and
trampled all over his feet. My palms sweated and I kept my
head turned away from his face. But he was awkward too,
and all at once he asked me to marry him. Just like that,
simple . . . no preambles. I was taken aback, yet he persisted, demanding an answer. I remained silent. He began to
explain his financial situation, along with his views on life.
It seemed he would try to tell me all about himself before
the dance ended. Yet I remained deaf. I thought how the
heat of the African sun must drive people off their sanity.
Suddenly, my uncle's behavior stopped appearing so

strange. This man dancing with me was just the same. It seemed as if everyone I met in this country was infected by the same spreading disease.

Does the émigré become abnormal once he has departed his own land? The man dancing with me insists on an answer before the end of the dance. I remain deaf and mute.

After we were home again, my uncle asked jealously, "What was Majed saying to you?" When I told him, he frowned. "How dreadful. Did he really ask you like that, without warning? I'm afraid Majed has no finesse. What was your reply?"

I said, "Nothing."

I sat in bed, the covers over me despite the heat. I wanted to be clear in my mind. What was I to do with my life after Africa? Where would I go? The day must come when I marry and my husband discovers that I am no longer a virgin, that I have undergone two abortions. It was not to sightsee or to get to know my uncle better that I have come to Africa, though these were the reasons I gave so insistently when I first urged him to invite me. (Only now do I see how it was my letters asking him to invite me to Africa that had prompted him to behave as he did.) Now I am in Africa because I want to be far from Beirut.

My father had begun to insist that I should marry Samir, Ahmad's friend, who had several times asked me to marry him. Each time I had refused, even though I liked him. But my father would ask, leaning over my shoulder like an ogre, "I only wish to know why on earth Samir wants to marry you? What does he see in you? You, with your drawn cheeks and pimpled, pock-marked face?" I felt like answering by telling him, "He wants to marry me because I am docile, because he has never seen my teeth, because I do not

rival his own self-importance, because I am a mystery to
him." Instead of explaining all this, however, I simply said,
"I will not marry, ever!"

My mother would shriek, "You will become an old
maid! Already you are an old maid! Buck up and accept
before he changes his mind." My answer was always the
same, "I will not marry, ever!" Calmly my father would ask
again, probing for a reason, "Zahra, if there is someone else
who wants to marry you, do not be afraid. Tell us." I keep
the answer deep within me. I hold Malek far away. I hold
the narrow bed in the garage room where he has lain on top
of me far away. I hold the picture of his wife and child,
which he always carries in his wallet, and which I have
glimpsed when he pays for coffee in that café frequented
only by those afraid to be seen together in public, far away.

I hold the thought of him away from my body, which
never once responded to his or experienced ecstasy, as I
pushed away the hand of the old doctor who worked to
abort my pregnancy. I erase from my mind my return home
after the abortion when I kept my feet and thighs pressed
tightly together so that my father would not discover my
secret. I even hold away the chair which knows me so well
in the café where I went with Malek many times and where
he first set about my seduction by speaking of friendship.
Whoever has a face and body like mine is easily persuaded;
or that was how I later rationalized my actions. He said how
much he liked my face with its pimples, how the disfigura-
tions actually excited him, even as he lay on top of me,
penetrating my virginity.

As for me, I felt only that I was like the other girls I
knew, someone with bigoted parents. But my father's image, coming into my mind, frightened me to the extent
where I felt sure he would kill me should he ever find out.

He would not hesitate, I knew, even if it meant him spending the rest of his life in prison. He was capable of severing my head from my body. I tried to dismiss all those images that, even so, kept haunting me as Malek brought his moving inside me to a conclusion and then waited for me to leave the garage room, which belonged to one of his friends, so he also could leave. Never once did he mention a future, or even a present.

The last time that I left the Al-Régie government tobacco factory and saw him nodding his head at me, indicating I should follow, I felt sick but followed nevertheless. It was as if he had a magnetic attraction which I could not resist. As I came closer to him, a wave of coldness swept over me. I was shivering even though my head and ears were covered. My feet were damp from the morning rain. My back grew rigid, my lips dry. I thought of the pimples sitting on them, refusing to disappear since the day of the abortion.

I came up to him as he stood waiting. He got into the car and leaned across to open the door to let me in. Yet I never told him how ill I felt. I sat still, trying to stop my body from shuddering, my teeth from rattling. He stopped the car and, as usual, disappeared ahead into the building. I didn't hold back nor for one minute consider not joining him, despite the sensation of hardly being able to move or walk. I entered the familiar building, looking over my shoulder, took two steps towards the garage, which appeared deserted, and dismissed an impulse to take refuge in one of the parked cars. There was no sound except for my footsteps until I entered the room tucked away at the end of the building. As I went in at the half-open door, I felt the coldness again. Again my teeth chattered.

He took hold of both my hands and sat me down on the

one piece of furniture in the room: the bamboo bed with its
stained yellow bed-cover. And I shivered, just as I had shivered the first time he brought me here. I shivered every
time and had no idea why I continued coming. He had
begun it at our first meeting by speaking of friendship. How
wonderful it had been to meet over a cup of coffee and hear
how he despised those conventions which allowed no room
for friendship between "Adam and Eve."

At our second meeting, he told me how he had found
me a job as a typist in the Al-Régie factory in the city's
suburbs. My brother had sent me along to his real-estate
office one morning to get him to find me work. I hesitated
before going, but only a little, for Malek was a friend of
Ahmad's and a friend of the family. He would call in each
evening with Ahmad, bringing with him a package containing either eggs or tomatoes or ground meat. Every evening
they brought in their dinners and he and Ahmad sat in the
kitchen, eating and laughing.

At our third meeting, he spoke of love, of Khalil Gibran
and platonic affection. He cursed marriage and children, not
forgetting to mention that, while he had hoped he might
marry me, my silence had not encouraged him.

During our fourth meeting, he held my hand and di-
verted the waiter so as to steal a secret kiss. I accepted everything that happened, listened to him and said very little,
for I was afraid to be seen with him in public. The sound of
every passing footstep was agonizing. Every chance voice
was like a needle pricking my flesh. Yet I never refused anything he asked, all the while saying very little. When he first
suggested the room in the garage, I tried to object. He soon
convinced me. The idea of the garage was because he
wished to safeguard my reputation. No one ought to see me
in the company of a married man.

When we entered the garage for the first time, it seemed he had swallowed his tongue and, along with it, the eulogies on platonic love and Khalil Gibran's famous quotations. He began kissing me; as I remained passive I could only think of the safety pin which held my brassiere strap together and hoped he wouldn't feel it; and that he wouldn't notice the run in my stockings; and of how from today I should check that my underpants are always clean. He wasn't at all vexed by my passivity while he was kissing me or as he made love to me. When, afterwards, I saw the blood, the proof of my virginity, on my thighs and on the yellow coverlet, I said to him, "Swear before God that we are married. It is all I ask." But he wouldn't speak the words: "I have married you." He explained his reasons to me. He didn't wish to tie me down, to stand in my way. One lecture followed another about equality between men and women, about what the true significance was of a good relationship . . . all kinds of things. And I still said very little. His refusal had no effect on our relationship since I went on seeing him day after day: there, in the same small room at the rear of the garage. He even brought our meetings in the café to a stop, canceled the car rides, forgot many of his speeches. I still shiver today when I think how I believed it was possible for me to control him and our relationship after my pregnancy and abortion. I thought I could influence him; that was my delusion. He would meet me and kiss me, and I would push him away. Then he would lift my skirt casually, not even bothering to undress me completely before making love to me. All at once I would be filled with disgust and contempt . . . the same feelings that had come over me during the abortion.

The old doctor had made me lie down with the help of a rather fat elderly nurse who fixed her hair and put on her lipstick without the aid of a mirror. I thought she was a hallucination, that I was still under the effects of anaesthesia. Yet there she stood before me, combing her hair and outlining her mouth with lipstick. I turned away from her and prayed to God never to see the woman again in my life, never to run into her again and have her find out I was not married. After the operation, she kept saying, "Come along, ducky, your husband will miss you. Come along, my honey."

She wanted me to leave as soon as possible, but I was still wobbly, the anaesthetic still completely numbed me, and I kept my face turned away from her so she wouldn't be able to recognize me again. I wanted her to forget forever how I looked. But it was a vain hope! I saw her two more times. Once when I went to try to have my virginity restored, and again when I returned once more after Malek had undone the doctor's handiwork in one split second, without it being any pleasure to him since he knew the restoration was counterfeit.

"Uncle, please tell me why you have stretched out by my side." Oh, how I wish I could have said those words! "Uncle, if you could hear the beat of my heart, if you could only see the disgust and fury gathered in my soul. If only you knew what my true feelings were. I am at my wits' end, and am annoyed with myself and hate myself because I stay silent. When will my soul cry out like a woman surrendering to a redeeming love?"

I stayed motionless. I remained expressionless. It was as if I were dead, even as a battle raged inside me, from the top of my head to the tips of my toes, and left devastation in its wake. Then he came closer and took my hand, which still carried faint menstrual traces on the nails, left there when I had checked in the night to see whether my period had begun. As he started to lick my fingers, he noticed a strange taste, but drew closer, saying how sharply he longed for his family. At that point, even through his trousers and my nightgown, I felt his penis throbbing against my thigh. I shuddered, opened my mouth to try to speak, to cry, to threaten, to protest, but instead found myself merely mumbling, "Why don't you let me sleep?"

I got out of bed, feeling very upset. It was as if it was only his waking me each morning that disturbed me, not his manner in general. I ran to the bathroom piled with television sets and sat there crying in a voice that might have been heard all over Africa.

As I buried my head in my hands and closed my eyes, I saw myself back with my mother in the straw booth, half-asleep, scratching my mosquito bites. I was afraid to open my eyes in case my hands, contaminated with fig juice, might redden my eyes. There was a sound of whispering and a movement on the only mattress, laid on the floor, which I shared with my mother. As I felt a movement and heard another voice, I bent my face close to my body and, pressing my legs to my chest, tucked my hands under my chin. Once my whole body was huddled in this way, the movement subsided. I froze in my position and slept.

When I awoke, my mother's man friend was outside the booth, sipping coffee. That night, as I slept, I was again awoken by noise and voices. As I huddled myself into a ball, the movement subsided, but now I stayed wide awake in a pool of perspiration that seeped into and soaked the mattress. My eyes were bloodshot. I was short of breath. My palms bled from my nails having dug into them. I was unable to meet my mother's eye or to look at the man in the booth next door to Mustapha's.

I lifted my head at the sound of knocks on the narrow

bathroom door and my uncle's voice, but I felt as though anything taking place outside that door could be nothing to do with me. I rested my head back on my hands, sensing a seeping, enveloping warmth. Once again, there was my mother's pale round face, a dimple on her chin, her eyes blue, her hair fair. There were her plump hands, her blue silk dress, the black veil which masked her features. I saw him and her together in the mountains, "close to the walnut tree." At times I saw myself kicking at the vines with my shoes until the grapes fell as her lover ran, holding me up in his arms and squeezing me and staring at the bruises on my thigh. I saw her in her full house-dress, sitting on the floor, her head in his arms. I watched her show photographs to her friend, for whom I never cared. My mother laughed as, anxiously and timidly, she held the pictures. I saw her in another photograph, being carried away in his arms. I searched for myself in that picture, but couldn't find that I was there, even though I recognized the walnut tree and the clean brown stones.

The knocking at the door and my uncle's voice both persisted. Slowly I lifted my head and pressed it to the wall as if neither sound had anything to do with me. I held my head as if to form a cocoon whose narrow walls would enfold me with love. I had no idea of how much time was passing.

I only looked up again when I saw how the door was being destroyed and almost falling in on top of me, and how my uncle was beside me, the veins standing out on his face and hands.

"What have you done to yourself?" He shook me. "What have you done?"

The room was encased in silence—as though nothing had ever happened. I kept my eyes down, remained seated on the bathroom stool and then stood up like a sleepwalker.

Nothing disturbed me. I no longer heard my uncle's voice, nor even his footsteps behind me. I couldn't even see him. It seemed as if I continued to sleep, whether I walked or stood. After a while, I found myself back in bed, as my uncle waited at its side with another man. I felt pain in my hand, but couldn't lift a finger. The other man was attempting to ask me questions in French. I couldn't understand a thing. He left the room, followed by my uncle.

How many days went by? How many nights? I cannot say. Time had cheated me; Africa had cheated me. I felt the heat despite the air conditioning, and saw through the windows how the sky was grey. I noticed how the birds had taken refuge in the clouds and tree-tops. The flies were constantly pleading with the netting that covered the windows and doors, begging to be let in, if only for a minute. My uncle was seated. I couldn't move my lips. His black servant carried away a tray. The doctor was searching for my wrist under the covers. As if in a trance, I knew nothing except for the light prick of a needle in my hand. It hurt. I was unable to lift my hand. My uncle's voice was pleading. I was quite surprised that he should ask me to speak. Didn't he realize that was impossible? I tried to speak. I could not form a word.

Whenever I felt on the verge of losing control over my bladder, I would grope my way out of bed quietly. Going to the bathroom, I might catch sight of myself in the mirror, stand stock still and gasp. There was my red face, there my swollen lips. Back under the covers, I would rest, staring at my uncle, who could not get one word out of me as I lay on that eternal bed. The scene outside remained the same: flies at the window net, birds swooping, tree-tops, grey skies. After many days I recalled Majed's request to marry me, an idea I had tried to dismiss. Now it reasserted itself in my mind, perhaps because I was in a state where everything existed yet didn't exist. Who could blame me? I felt in an unusual frame of mind.

It was how I had felt in Beirut after I found out that I was pregnant for the second time and Malek had been going into the best date for my abortion with the old doctor and his nurse. I saw Malek's mouth move and heard his voice clearly, but didn't take in what he was saying and couldn't manage to discover what it was. I sat relaxed, my eyes grown used to how the garage room looked, as though my fate was irrevocable. There was no escaping from the room. I remained motionless. I tried, unsuccessfully, to remember why I was here. I knew Malek's face and body, but had no idea what he was talking about. It was as if the din of the passing traffic had reached a pitch where it was so enmeshed in my hearing that I could no longer pick out the words he spoke. I tried again, but by this time Malek was addressing me angrily. His wide eyes apparently narrowed. I tried to get my thoughts together and to concentrate on what he said, but I could not manage it. I had forgotten what we were discussing; anything to do with me remained a blank.

I sat with frightened eyes, alternately staring at door and floor. I was aware he had taken hold of me, forced me into the car and then into the doctor's clinic. I felt a sharp pain in my lower abdomen. No sooner had I closed my eyes on the image of the nurse than I found myself back in our house with my mother crying. She had tucked her hair up under a white kerchief as I lay dozing fitfully.

I saw Malek standing at my mother's side, talking to her as she wept. I wondered where my father had got to. The anaesthetic had not yet worn off. It occurred to me to ask where my father was each time I opened my eyes, but the thought disappeared whenever I closed them again. They took me next to a hospital in the city where a doctor spoke to me for hours, though I don't recall answering any of his questions. I did, however, memorize the hospital's daily routine. I obeyed every order. My own voice only returned momentarily after they had run their electric current through every cell in my body, every bone, every drop of blood. I thought I would never escape from the state I was in. It was hard to believe I ever could, as they jolted me against my will and my tongue stayed imprisoned in its housing of plastic. Yet those electric shocks would eventually return me to being myself and help me to get back to my job at the factory and live a normal life in all respects as if nothing had happened, as though it was some other woman, not I, who had been for a spell in hospital.

The one difference afterwards was that my father's attitude towards me altered. He became friendlier. My mother was meanwhile worried that I might tell people I had been in a mental hospital. She hoped I'd conceal the fact that I'd been given ECT. She questioned me constantly about how many people might have seen me breaking down at work before the boss contacted Malek. My mother chattered on about it all as I became filled with disgust at Malek's lies and deceits.

In Africa, once I was out of bed again and had begun to get my appetite back, I thought all the time about Majed's proposal. I plotted how I might trick him and so get round his discovering that I was a woman who had twice been aborted. The problem caused me many restless days and nights. No day dawned, in any case, when I didn't open my eyes to see the sun or the rain and feel scared stiff that my father might sometime find out the truth. I comforted myself periodically with the fancy that nature would never let him learn my secret; that nature, knowing his fierce charac-

ter, would shield me. I never asked myself whether my fear
of my father was on a mental or a physical level. It was all
part of a conglomeration of fear, of fear, above all, that my
image of myself might be overturned . . . the image of
which I had run off hundreds of copies for distribution to
all who had known me since childhood. Here is Zahra, the
mature girl who says little; Zahra the princess, as my grandfather dubbed me; Zahra the stay-at-home, who blushes for
any or for no reason; Zahra the hard-working student—
quite the reverse of her brother, Ahmad; Zahra, in whose
mouth butter would not melt, who has never smiled at any
man, not even at her brother's friends. This is Zahra—a
woman who sprawls naked day after day on a bed in a stink-
ing garage, unable to protest at anything. Who lies on the
old doctor's table . . .

When I came back from the market place I said to my
uncle, as perspiration drenched my body, "I shall accept
Majed's proposal."

He blurted out, "Have you met him in the market?"

I shook my head. I did not know what was passing in my
uncle's mind, since he stayed silent. But when I asked him
what he thought about it, "Good," he said in a low voice,
and added, "Although are you certain you'll want to live
with him in a small village, far from the capital, as Majed
has planned?"

I nodded.

My uncle left the room briefly, and when he came back
took hold of my hand. I withdrew it as a reflex. Yet he
asked me to sit and listen to him carefully, since, for the first
time, he wished to place me face to face with my situation.

"Listen, I can speak to you, since we are not strangers to
each other. These fits which come over you are no slight
matter. Majed must be told about your condition before

you marry. It cannot be otherwise. Don't misunderstand me. You're an intelligent, normal girl, but the doctor has told me these fits are not a simple thing. Majed must be told, since we are a good and honorable family. We should hide nothing from him."

In an ostrich's voice I replied, as my heart beat wildly, "Whatever happened to me was your fault!"

"My fault?" He stared at me and asked hysterically, "My fault? How can you say such a thing, Zahra?"

Once again, in my ostrich's voice, not knowing how the words escaped, I replied, "Yes. Your fault. Perhaps you didn't intend it, but I never cared for your behavior towards me."

He yelled back, "What are you saying, girl? What behavior?"

Again in the ostrich's voice, "At the movies, when you held my hand. In the mornings, when you slept by my side. It troubled me until it made me sick."

He stood up and went out of the room without looking back. I heard the door slam. He had left me alone, trembling with my confession.

3

Uncle

I walked on the unpaved ground, holding pen and paper, trying to phrase a cable to my sister, Fatmé, and my brother-in-law, Ibrahim, to inform them about Zahra's forthcoming wedding.

The laughter of the Africans held me. They were getting drunk now, as they had yesterday, and do each night. The beer bottles with tall thin necks lift across their faces and empty down their throats. When blacks drink, they drink the whole world. They take pleasure in drinking to the extent where they reach a state of being and non-being. Is that happiness? Yet there remains something disturbing which cannot be defined. Their music beats out a monotonous rhythm. The beat sounds echoes down their throats, engulfs their world. I see them at the back of my street in their open-sided bamboo cane hut, swaying and emptying bottles into their mouths; swaying and falling down on the ground. When they get up they laugh endlessly.

"Why do they drink?" I ask myself. "Is it because they

can't discover the creator of these tall, dense trees? Is it because the burning sun makes them perpetually thirsty? Or is it because the colors of their designs dazzle the eyes? Or because there is in Africa a green flower?"

When I arrived here and breathed the air for the first time, I held my head high and thought, "How wonderful it is to breathe! How beautiful is freedom!" Ignoring the waves of hot air that rose to meet me, I stepped down on to the hot asphalt of the airport.

Streams of water ran between the slender trees. The clothes which draped the black bodies were colored, decorated with dried grasses and shells. Some bodies slept lazily beside the streams. Others stood about, while still others sat casually.

You were my choice, Africa! I preferred you to Brazil or Jordan because I had been dreaming of you since my tender childhood. I dreamed of your elephants, of your colors, your drum-beats. There were those eternal designs on ivory in my sister Ilham's house. I would draw close to them, to place my lips on them so that I might feel of what they were made. The material was quite like wood, yet it wasn't wood; something like stone, but not quite stone. Whenever I saw an airline commercial, saw naked breasts dancing or men's feet stepping to the beat of a drum as their teeth shone white, I would tell myself, "How I wish to have my woman lying down and sleeping as the drums beat and I fan her with an ostrich-feather fan, peel pineapples for her and hold a coconut to her lips. I want to hear the voices of the jungle with her, and see Tarzan and Cheeta themselves."

I could hardly explain any of this to my comrades in the party when the forged passport arrived, with the one-way ticket to Africa, after our *coup d'état*. "Nothing will change for you," they said. "Most of your relatives were in Africa

long before the *coup*. Now you will be joining them quite
naturally and not as if the police were after you." I nodded
my head, as though in agreement. Their nerves were also
shattered as we sat in that dark Damascus hotel.

Their hands would go to their guns the moment a tama-
rind seller crashed his cymbals in the street. Their pupils
would move from left to right, up and down, whenever
they heard wooden clogs on the stairs. They would hold
their breath when the telephone rang in reception and its
echo reached the third floor. Any steps approaching our two
rooms would prompt Issam to put on his fake glasses, Riad
to grab up his woollen hat and me to go and stand behind
the door, my gun hidden behind my back, my finger on its
trigger. At those critical moments our nerves were like bee
hives as fear mixed with reality, hallucination with courage.
That was how we were until sleep crept up despite all our
resistance and we abandoned ourselves to it completely as
though the possibility of arrest had suddenly become of no
concern.

I was the only one who remained for hours without
growing impatient. I would sit and imagine that I was hugging Louise and Mary whose face was painted like a peacock's tail. I would sit and draw the "Red Storm" on paper.
I had hung this emblem on our living-room wall, despite
my mother's protest, and here I would also kiss the portrait
of Saadeh, our founder. I had hung the map of "Greater
Syria" next to my sister Wafaa's diploma, awarded to her for
excellence in reciting the Qur'an. I would dream that I was
talking to the wife of the founder, who was First Secretary
of the party, or riding in a car with his three daughters. I
couldn't embrace them, but I was happy to be sitting next
to them. I would hear the party anthem "Syria Is Great"
being repeated, and I would gather all my strength to shout

out the slogans at every meeting: "To whom is life, O sons of life?" and they would answer in one voice: "To us!" And I would cry out again: "To what is our allegiance?" "To Syria!" they would answer. "Who is our leader?" "Saadeh! Saadeh! Saadeh!"

I would gather our family's children, boys and girls, Zahra among them, and ask them to memorize the party's charter and principles for half a lira each a page. My eyes would fill with tears as I wished Saadeh could be alive to hear those young hearts repeating his words.

My three comrades were talking. Two wanted a woman, while the third said we shouldn't take risks. I went to the closet and took out the walking stick and leather bag. As I left the room, Issam had begun talking about how essential it was that I should tell him where I was going. I didn't answer, but set off down the dirty stairs. At each step I could smell the stench from the rest-rooms. Paint was peeling from the walls in flaky layers. I suddenly realized that I was holding the walking stick instead of leaning on it. I wondered whether my fake limp would succeed in drawing attention to my feet rather than to my face. My photographs had been in all the Lebanese papers. There was one picture of me in downtown Beirut, performing the party salute, and another showing me barechested, admiring the muscles in my arms, which I had developed like a body builder's. How did the newspapers get hold of those pictures on the eve of the *coup d'état,* the same night that the investigators entered our house as my sister Wafaa sat on the floor at her studies? She had begun to shout "Thief!" but the investigators didn't trouble to correct her. They just snatched the book out of her hands and turned it over. They searched all the rooms and every inch of the house. They questioned my mother about my whereabouts. Innocently, she led them to my room, showed them the bed made up. One of them asked, "Do you think I am stupid? Come on! Tell us! Where is Hashem?"

She shook her head, crying, "I swear by God, my cousins, I do not know."

They continued to ask about Abu Hashem.

"In the south, in Nabatiya," she answered.

Sarcastically one of them commented, "You don't know about your son, but you know where your husband is."

"No one ever asks where Hashem goes or what he does," she replied.

They searched the rooms meticulously, as if looking for a needle in a haystack, I was later told. Not a page of my sister's books was left unexamined. One of them then ordered the others up on to the roof, which linked up with neighboring rooftops. They all disappeared in their long raincoats, wearing hats and carrying guns. Two remained on guard outside the door.

Then my mother and sister gathered together everything in my closet, all my books and papers, and fed them into the bathroom stove after lighting it. As they grew more frightened, so they became more frantic, throwing everything they could find into the flames, including my spectacles case. The smell of burning leather filled the house.

At this point there came from the stove the loud report of a shot, closely followed by another. The investigators began to shout, "Some swine's opened fire on us. Where is the bastard?" Two investigators began to search the house all over again, and were joined by others who waved their guns and yelled, "We heard shots. There's a smell of gunfire." Tracking down the source of the smell to the bathroom stove, they saw the books and papers burning there and gave my mother a look of disdain and doubt. One of them tried to put out the fire and retrieve the half-burned books and papers as he deluged my mother and sister with insults. He quietened down when he saw two spent cartridge cases among the charred books.

The investigators visited my home on three consecutive days. Once they took my mother away for questioning. Another time they took Wafaa and repeatedly asked her what she had been doing after midnight in the living room on the day of the *coup d'état;* for whom had she been waiting; when had she last seen her brother, and what had he told her? Other investigators stayed for a whole week at my father's booth in the south. Perhaps they expected to see my face pop out from behind the green tobacco leaves.

The last time I saw Wafaa she was carrying two knitting needles and standing, as usual, with other girls by an alley wall. No sooner did she see me than she tried to run away, for I had forbidden her ever to go and play in the alley or rub lemons on the wall. I wanted her to be like Saadeh's daughters, like Raghida, whom I had never seen without a book in her hands as she sat out in the garden, not like the other girls in our quarter. As I looked fiercely at her she trembled. "I wasn't playing. I am knitting. Mother said I could." I tugged her black braids, then let her go and took a lira out of my pocket. On that fateful day I smiled and never stopped walking, even though I kept looking over my shoulder to see the look on her face because I hadn't scolded her.

She ran to catch up with me, joined me and held out her hand. I gave her the lira as we walked. I was on the verge of saying something, but hesitated. Instead I ran up to my room to change my clothes. Looking for my mother, I found her in the kitchen, embraced and kissed her as she, in her surprise, kept asking why I was so happy. I answered: "Today is New Year's Eve!"

I heard her saying: "God have mercy. Years have gone by and I never even realized it. I came here, and your father is still in the village."

I went back to my room purposelessly and thought, "I shall be leaving today or tonight." I thought of the words scattered about in my comrades' notebooks, labeled with their code-names, "Adonis," "Malkart." After tonight there would be no more party meetings, no more sessions or futile words. Despite all the fiery slogans, colors fade in the end and pages turn yellow.

After Saadeh was executed, my commitment to the party changed its form. I can still remember how I burst out crying and rushed to all the party meetings, to all the regional centers, asking why they hadn't set the world ablaze. How could things stay the same? How could the air, the water, the movie marquees, the din of tram and honking of taxis remain unchanged? How could the vegetable vendors still go about their business? How could we still breathe? Was not Saadeh the party, the party Saadeh? Saadeh was murdered, the party was therefore murdered.

Yet, even so, life did go on. I would sit at meetings with my head bowed before giving angry cries as tears choked me. When it came to the chairman asking, "Are there any questions?" I would have questions ready which were nothing to do with the evening's topic. As he nodded his head and in an authoritative voice commanded, "Speak, comrade," the order, delivered in Classical Arabic, would make me feel euphoric, like a real general in a real army.

I would stand up and begin with well-rehearsed words. "We must do something. We must not only write down what takes place in our meetings, and debate with and persuade others. We need to act. We need to rage like a bush fire throughout this system which has put our leader in his grave."

In my anger I would observe myself threatening, pointing an accusing finger. The words would pour out of me, propelled by my saliva. The chairman would try to calm me: "We understand, Comrade Hashem, Comrade Hashem." It was not just once or twice but perhaps a hundred times that, after entering the party, I felt like a grenade ready to explode at any moment.

It was my cousin Hassan who introduced me to the party. At one time he headed the student group at the American University in Beirut. He would talk and talk and I listen and not understand a word. He spoke of a Greater Syria, of the Fertile Crescent. With all my eighteen years, I debated the issues. "Why should we care about other countries? Why don't we just worry about our own country and eradicate its hunger and poverty?" He would answer that, if all believed in a Greater Syria and a Fertile Crescent, then our own country's problems would be solved automatically. One of the first principles which I grasped was non-sectarianism. It attracted me like a magnet; I followed its course like an arrow. I was probably able to understand and justify any contradictions except religious differences.

I thanked my destiny and Hassan for having introduced me to this stimulating new world whose enthusiasms had made me into a man with a cause. These enthusiasms and their powerful currents drew me, as they did most of Lebanon. There was hardly a home which did not have its committed advocate, while, in schools and government institutions, men, women and children would repeat the party's slogans in unison.

I could not make myself be patient, like other comrades. I needed to listen and debate so that I could go out and spread the party's teachings among my acquaintances. I wanted to be truly committed, to create change, to fulfill every principle there and then. Some thought me unhinged.

One day Hassan told me: "You belong to a party with principles, a party that grows and develops, a party that will survive for future generations. That should be the great gain."

I asked: "So what? Here am I and there are you and the other party members. What of them?" I asked questions about the parties which belonged to the opposition. "How can we meekly accept them, the Lebanese Phalangists, the Liberal Socialists, the Najada? How can we live when these parties, which contradict everything we stand for, also live and grow?"

I once told Hassan that we should begin by assassinating the leaders of other parties. He took me aside and bluntly told me: "Hashem, you do not belong to a bunch of gangsters. You belong to an organized political party." And he added angrily, trying to make me understand: "Maybe I should have let you grow up before introducing you to the party and its principles. Don't let me wonder whether I made a mistake."

His words surprised me, as did his way of thinking. I answered that he seemed to look on the party just as any housewife might: everything in its proper place, everything well studied; a day for washing, a day for ironing, a day for sleeping together.

Hassan would accuse me of exaggerated party loyalty and political hooliganism. I stopped both discussing anything with him and questioning anyone else and began to think about what I really wanted to achieve. I once mentioned that I would like to visit a sports club which belonged to the Phalangists. The group fell silent, but the director said he had no objection. So I began to go there and, whenever I crossed the threshold into that Phalangist territory, my heart began to beat furiously. Before long, I was wearing gym shorts and lifting weights. And every time that I heard the hard breathing of the exercising Phalangists, I felt a hatred and contempt for them. I wanted to bring all their weights down on top of them and to see them shattered on the floor of their own club.

After a while, a Phalangist suggested to me that I should familiarize myself with the principles of the Lebanese Phalangists. This never came about because one of them spotted me in company with a comrade of my own party. Both lived in the same quarter. The Phalangist glared at me with eyes of fire.

I had by then submitted my report to the party, and so thereafter steered well clear of the Phalangist Club. The main communication I had had with the Phalangists had been when they asked me, as I lifted weights, whether I loved God, the fatherland and the family. When I nodded, one of them said, laughing, "You are a Phalangist without even knowing it!"

My report showed how the Phalangists were more interested in sports training and physical fitness than we were. Their propaganda was, moreover, easy and uncomplicated, in contrast to the obscure jargon exchanged by my PPS comrades, who used words I couldn't understand most of the time. After I left the Phalangist Club, I once again felt about to explode and most unlike any housewife. Hassan had been right when he said to me, "You want to justify your party membership while camouflaging the fact that you are really committed because you suffer from a whole bundle of inferiority complexes. You never completed your college education, you are unable to engage in any discussion which demands more than an instinctive intelligence." Hassan thought he could shut me up by talking in this way, but in fact he prompted me to engage all the more in endless debates at meetings, my line always revolving around the idea that action ought to be taken.

We should grasp our conflicts and collisions with other parties . . . we should begin working for "Greater Syria." All other Arab régimes should be brought down, one by one. We should liquidate the clergy and sheikhs, who use religion as a façade and a mirror behind which to hide as they spread their fanaticism like flashing reflections. Anyone who stands in the way of our national ambitions should be assassinated, even including those who belong to no party but who are nevertheless corrupt, who seek, through their corruption, to divide and weaken our people.

My cousin Hassan led a rally at the American University in Beirut, at which the voices of the young rose in a crescendo, all committed, all enthusiastic. I, too, shouted and exploded, but went even further. I accused the party of cowardice for never taking the initiative in any action. They did not know the meaning of discipline. How could the death of Saadeh be so forgotten? Why didn't they act? The question was anticipated, as was the answer: "We fear the party would then be hunted down, and that must be avoided. It would create too many problems." It was maybe my insistence and volatility which goaded them into making an attempt on the life of the judge, Yusuf Sharbal, who had ordered Saadeh's execution. When I read of the incident in the papers, I was beside myself with a mixture of elation and anger. How could they have thought of carrying out this decision without also considering me as the executioner?

Was I considered to be merely a "mouth" which sounded off? Was I thought of as one who walked with bent back and trembling hands? Did they imagine me to be already so contented with myself that such an added happiness would be altogether too much? I did not know. My elation mixed with anger began to distill itself into a white-hot blazing rage. If I had been the one delegated to the mission, then that bullet would have been fatal. They had planned it so as not really to kill him. I raised my protests during a meeting. My words were peppered with saliva which flew through the air and landed on their papers.

I hungered for adventure and risk. I cultivated defiance so that everyone would know I did so for the sake of the party. I wanted everyone to place their hearts on their sleeves. I sought to infiltrate Jumballat's Socialist Party and learn what its members thought, and how their meetings were run, so that later we could combat them. I did this secretly, since I feared the PPS comrades might expel me if they knew.

Eventually I mentioned the secret of my attending the Socialist Party gatherings to Hassan, and he, in turn, brought it up at a meeting, questioning whether such an act could be at all beneficial. I sat there, expecting to be thrown out, sweating with anxiety, but found they never went beyond a threat of expulsion. At that point they were too convinced of my loyalty and enthusiasm, but Hassan, as usual, took me aside to lecture me on how he had introduced me into the party and how I should therefore watch every step and word. He couldn't tolerate any more of my hooliganism. My love for the party looked like nothing more than impulsiveness.

Was it that the formidable energy I showed on the party's behalf bothered him? How could he say that I didn't understand the principles by which it functioned? How could he

question my motives for joining? I had joined the party so
that we could transform our compatriots and make them
into better citizens, so that we could unite and stand as one
against our common foes!

Hassan would answer, "Here is the real point. Conviction
is not enough. You, like all the young, are obsessed with
dreams of power and force. You joined the party thinking it
was a boxing match. You should be completing your college
education."

My anger welled up till I wished I could actually hit him.
I clenched my fist hard as I resisted the desire to strike out.
Was he asking me to leave the party and return to my books
and desk and all that stupidity because I had no true understanding of the party manifesto?

If only Hassan could have seen me then: Hashem Aloush,
delegated, with two comrades, to enter the residence of
President Shihab and place him under arrest. I, Hashem
Aloush, assigned to that mission as part of the *coup d'état*
which was to take place on the same night. It was a *coup*
designed to disarm the beliefs of those who claimed we
were a fascist group, since we would decline to take over
government once our *coup* had succeeded. We wished to
free Lebanon from Shihab and his military régime. That was
all. We would not govern. We would show them that it was
not glory and power which we sought. Let others govern. It
was democratic rule which we worked for.

Ah, Hassan, my enthusiasm, stubbornness and persistence
were no passing whims. When they racked their brains to
decide on the best person to arrest Fouad Shihab, it was I,
Hashem Aloush, who was delegated to give Shihab the
command, "Please follow me," once my comrades had
pinned down and paralyzed the Republican Guard.

With guns in our belts and cigarettes in our mouths and smoke pouring from our nostrils, we drove through the night towards zero hour. I held in my mind the image of my mother's face. Each one of us was tense. The secret password had not yet been given, but the radio was glued to my ear as we awaited the first bulletin which would inform us that all was going to plan. Perhaps all of Lebanon's clocks would stop simultaneously. Perhaps that would be the signal. Our car stood out like a torch in the night desert, conspicuous despite its routine make and color. Looking to left and right, I felt there were eyes on us, even though the road was deserted. It was as if everyone must know we were on a mission to get Shihab. I cried out to Kamal, behind the wheel, "Watch out! We don't want an accident. Here we are, on a life-or-death mission, and you can't even drive!"

And then every eye was indeed on us at the army checkpoint which tried to stop us and which we ignored and which promptly opened fire. What did it mean, this sudden road-block and hail of bullets? They were setting out in pursuit. I shouted, "Don't stop! Step on the accelerator!"

We heard the siren of a motor-cycle on our tail. We could only think of speeding on and fulfilling our mission. I heard Kamal say, "Maybe we should have stopped. It might have been no more than a routine check."

Sarcastically I responded, "Routine check! What if they found our guns?"

He answered, "A routine check. 'Your identity card, young man. God be with you.'"

I didn't answer. The siren behind us grew louder. As Kamal looked back, I said, "Step on it, Kamal! We have got to get Shihab. Come on, Kamal, faster. Your car can lose them." I was bursting with elation in spite of the strain.

This was a night of destiny. If only every night of one's life could be filled with such tension: a motor-cycle in pursuit, a siren wailing and over the airwaves a song, "Rise, oh rise, my country," the anthem we sang at party meetings and on outings. Before I could give a thought to who was playing it, Kamal dropped his speed and said, "There is a car ahead, giving us the party's signal." I kicked him as if he were a cow and said, "Don't you realize it's a trap! A trap! Step on it, Kamal!"

When the car stopped at last, a face familiar from one of our meetings loomed out of the night. I heard the comrade speak the words which I dreaded hearing: "I'm sorry to say we've failed. Save yourselves and escape." After that I was out of control, with everything confused: voices, sounds, the noise of the siren, rifle shots. Our comrade emphasized his words: "We've failed. Save yourselves. Escape to Damascus. We'll take care of you there. Long live Syria!"

His car shot off, and as we followed I found myself screaming at Kamal, "Don't believe him! We'll complete our mission. Get to Shihab. We'll finish our plan. Get to Shihab. He'll soon be sitting in this car, right here!"

Kamal stopped and turned off the engine. Furious, I opened the passenger door, went round to the driver's side and pushed Kamal across the seat as he kept repeating, "We must discuss this logically, Hashem, Comrade Hashem!" But my hands were on the wheel, my foot already pressing down the accelerator. I must have been going very fast because Kamal's voice faded out and I could hear only horns blaring. The radio kept beating out the scheduled programs and there was no sign of a news bulletin. A popular songster kept singing, "The moon is on our doorstep with all its lanterns aglow." The nervous tremor of Kamal's words echoed in my ears: "Where are we going, for God's sake? We have party instructions. Be careful. The *coup d'état* has failed."

Party instructions! That was all they were good for: giving orders even after they'd failed. What was the point? How could they continue to give instructions? They would do better to commit mass suicide. The *coup* had failed. How could I continue to live afterwards, after I had been strutting around like a peacock in the party so that Hassan always advised, "Calm down, we don't want any daredevil acts." Again I heard Kamal's shaking voice: "Don't despair. The party's in good shape. The fact that we've received the message with such efficiency shows the party's holding strong."

His bleating gnaws at me and my foot presses down on the accelerator. We will storm the presidential palace in Junie, even though our supplies, meant for starting a confrontation with the guards, may have been intercepted.

I drove on until we came to a barricade, when I veered on to an unsurfaced road. In my fury I pressed the accelerator too hard and crashed the car across an unfenced garden hung with Christmas decorations. We reached a dead end as we stopped the car and got out to return the army's fire. Kamal's voice rang in my ears: "This is suicide, Comrade Hashem. It's suicide. Maybe it's not us they are after. Maybe it's another group they're fighting."

I pushed him aside: "Leave me alone. Don't stop me."

The firing came closer. There were only two houses and a few trees between us and the soldiers. Several shots ricocheted off the trees. Kamal, a mass of trembling sweaty words, stated, "I'm getting out, Comrade Hashem. I will not be a participant in your personal battle. It's suicide."

I didn't answer. I wasn't by then even aware of his presence. I heard the car engine start as I reloaded my gun in the darkness, and thought that, despite his caution, Kamal could fall into a trap through using the car. The firing died down as everything came to a standstill and suddenly returned to normal. Kamal's engine had fallen silent.

There were in the darkness, however, voices charged with anger which asked, "Who was with you? Answer, you bastard! How many persons?" I couldn't hear Kamal's answer, only the sound of a beating. They had arrested him. They were only a few meters away. Perhaps they were close behind me. It was suicide! How did I think I could take a whole barracks with my twenty-odd bullets? Perhaps the time had indeed come to head for Damascus and start preparing for another, better-organized *coup d'état*.

I began to run between houses and trees, to stumble up slopes. "Kamal, what a fool you were." I ran, but froze whenever I heard voices. No. They would never arrest me. I now knew one thing only: "Escape to Damascus." I found myself in a forest such as I had never known existed in Lebanon. There were huge trees where the flutterings of roosting birds drew my glances upwards. I went deep into the trees until I was immersed in their silence and darkness. It seemed as though Lebanon, the struggle and its failure had never touched this place. Now I must escape to Damascus where no one could touch me. I would not be able to return to Lebanon for a year or two. Perhaps that was why I had gone into my room to wish it good-bye, and had kissed my sister and mother in parting.

After walking for two hours, I saw the lights of moving cars. I weaved my way between rocks and left behind me the formidable trees and their silence broken only by the cries of birds. Cars kept passing in both directions, in spite of the late hour. It was still New Year's Eve. I paid no attention to where my feet landed, on which stones. While keeping my balance on soft sandy rocks which crumbled under pressure I had stumbled against thorns that lacerated my feet and thighs. The land sloped downwards and I could only take it one step at a time. There was a great commotion behind me. I turned, but could see nothing. I was surprised to find the asphalt road only a few meters away. Fear gripped me. I thought, "In a few seconds, I will leave this safe cover and be walking on asphalt. A few moments ago I thought only of thorns which bloodied my feet. Now, walking on asphalt, I think only of hiding. What am I to do when the highway lies wide open before me? It points to the sea and the rushing cars seem like counter-currents."

I walked close to the edge of the highway, one foot on the verge, the other on the tarmac. I walked close to the undergrowth so should someone challenge me I could return quickly to its cover. I turned up my shirt collar and buried my hands in my pockets as the cold wind began to sting my face. As I went I whistled a tune, as if feeling perfectly sure of myself and at peace with the world. A bus stopped directly next to me, and a woman with two children and a man climbed down. The man began to unload packages from the bus rack and I overheard him wish the bus driver, "God be with you." Just as the bus began to move again, I jumped into it, as I was used to doing on the tram-cars.

As I left my country I thought, "Is it true that we have an army which is capable of arresting, plotting and knowing everything about our party members, capable of tracking us all down?" I felt like crying as I recalled the party headquarters, my bed and, hanging above it, Saadeh's portrait with his sayings. I thought of my mother's footsteps as she went in her metal-heeled house slippers, beating a tattoo from kitchen to living room in spite of my having given instructions that no one was to interrupt our party meeting. My mother could never wait.

When I escaped across the border, I could not even kneel down with my face near the ground to taste the sand and say good-bye. If I had bitterly embraced a tree, an onlooker would have thought I was finding some kind of sexual gratification.

Words are warm things. I am full of memories. I remember lying naked on the roof of the house, following the doctor's instructions. The summer sun had to get to my body. My mother and my sister Wafaa and I used to go together to a farm which the doctor suggested when I was coughing so violently. We couldn't go south because the scent of green tobacco irritated my nose. I was frightened to sleep because of the coughing, in case my breathing stopped. Death, to me, meant closing my eyes and sleeping. How could I say good-bye to my country? If I said good-bye to each citizen in turn, shook hands, kissed and hugged them, would that be an adequate farewell? Warm memories must be my good-bye.

When I woke up one day and saw bright red spots of blood on the pillow, I called my mother. The blood made her think I was dying. She moaned, screamed and rushed on to the balcony. My aunt tried to calm down my mother, but she screamed: "Help! Send for Abu Hashem. Let him come at once." Then she moaned on, "I'd rather die than see him in Bihaness."

Years later I found out what she meant by "Bihaness." My mother's Uncle Mahdi arrived from the south, clutching his abdomen. When we asked him what the matter was he would reply, "There is a snake in my stomach. I swallowed it when I drank from a terracotta pitcher that contained river water. The snake must have been very tiny, for I didn't feel it at the time, but now it grows in my tummy, and grows and moves."

Whenever my great-uncle paid us a visit, it was as if a whole bundle of comic books had arrived in the house. His stories would make us laugh. He would refuse to enter if my mother was out. He would sit and wait on the steps among his bundles of clothing. He had no teeth. We would go up to him and ask him to guess who we were, and he would always be completely confused. It was very hard on him because the neighborhood children joined in as great-uncle tried to answer. As he smiled, showing his toothless gums, we would laugh louder and louder until he grew angry and hit out with his cane. Sometimes we would hide the cane from him. When he cursed us while chasing us, we also hid his clothes. In desperation he would begin to spit at us and say, "Shame on you!" Then his coughing began. We thought it was all an act, but my mother's uncle was suffering from tuberculosis without realizing it and spent his last days in the sanatorium at Bihaness.

Memories grow stronger after one leaves one's homeland. Memories belong to the past, but one wants them to be alive in the present, as glossy as my photographs showing my nephews and nieces, among them Zahra and Ahmad in Shaghour Hamana. We stand with our hands reaching out for the cold water. I remember the taste of that water to this day.

How was it possible for me to carry all those memories with me to Damascus and there recall them? Abd the hashish smoker, for instance, clear in my memory as he spoke to himself, smoked hashish and had fights with his mother. Abd would melt whenever he met a woman. He would gaze at her tenderly and tell her, "If you were to accept me in marriage, I would bedeck you in diamonds." It was said that Abd's father once owned all the buildings in the Bab Idriss district but lost them one by one. He sent his eldest son to America to study to be a doctor, but never saw or heard from him again. No news ever came back once the son waved good-bye, dressed in his new hat and suit, and sailed away from his parents and brother Abd. It was said that the father gambled and drank, and paraded women in front of his wife, while she consulted palmists and astrologers.

I never found out if the story were true, and never tried to. Along with the other boys, I was interested only in playing tricks on Abd, in making fun of him, especially if we could press him to the point of blasphemy. Although Abd would make us laugh out loud, he could also have us trembling for our lives in case he got hold of us.

Once, when the house was like an oven, I took my mattress up to sleep on the roof. My mother had gone south to visit my father. The boys from my quarter came up on to the roof and stayed from afternoon to evening. We grew hungry without thinking that we could have gone down into the house to eat. We sat on the rooftop, waiting for the relief of the cool evening, looking at passers-by and amusing ourselves by watching Abd walking with his head bent to his chest as his voice grew louder and louder as he talked to himself. Whispering, we agreed on a plan. I went down the wooden stairs and brought up the garbage container. Then we pelted Abd with its contents. As the rotting tomatoes and lime peels flew about him, he came to a standstill, finally realizing that he was a target. He couldn't spot us as we flattened ourselves behind the parapet.

Crawling to the other side of the roof, peeping from behind the line of laundry, I could see Abd fuming, cursing his creator and all humanity. No sooner did a washing-powder box hit him in the face than he looked up. We could hardly stifle our laughter, although we were terrified and lay still, holding our breath. As I lay with my eyes closed, I felt eyes boring into me. I held in my laughter, although it was difficult, and controlled my breathing as if I were genuinely asleep. But Abd, insisting on the truth and skeptical of my innocence, remained standing and panting, having climbed the stairs, although I hadn't heard his steps. He drew closer and closer, knowing me to be ring-leader.

I began trembling and to anticipate the moment when he would strike me. My mother had constantly warned me against taunting Abd, he being insane. I kept my eyes closed until he gave up and I heard his steps fading. I opened my eyes and kicked the other boys, who sat there silently.

I carry these memories with me as I carry my arm or my body. Perhaps the homeland is present and past together. Perhaps it is routine. One cannot love and grow used to a routine unless it is part of the reality of your homeland. In foreign countries, routine seems to become no more than a way of killing time until you return to your homeland. Everything you experience in your homeland has meaning and value because it is like the experience between son and father.

Here we can sit by a sea that resembles ours, whose waves, breaking on the rocks, sound the same as those at home. They, too, shift pebbles, leave wet sand behind. Here, on top of a high mountain, crickets chirp, and there are familiar red-tiled roofs. Here are cows being milked by a woman who uses the same kind of pail. Here are large apartments, small apartments, containing the same upholstery. Here we sit and speak of these people's past as if it is not perching here beside us. I wish I could have stayed close to the pots of basil beside my father's shed in the south. I miss the wrestling magazines, the sex magazines under my pillow, the kitchen tiles.

How long shall I remain in Africa, breathing its furnace air, tasting its odorless bread between black walls? Yet there is a constant smell of dampness in the trees and stones, even in the cobwebs. Whenever I meet someone newly arrived in this country, I notice that the dampness disappears. Then everything sparkles, the mornings become clear. But afterwards, little by little, the dampness returns, encloses. Soon the newly arrived becomes a part of Africa.

I never thought I would grow used to the heat, for every time I opened the door of my house and saw the sun I had a feeling of being trapped. The sun in Africa is not circular. It is surrounded by rays of differing lengths. I thought I would get over my feeling by walking to the big city square and moving from store to store. I would become a new person, learning to speak and think in a new language. The libraries remained empty. The mass of fire swam in its fixed position. These homes are not planned for comfort. I, too, seem to have caught this infection and to be living on a railway platform without walls or corners.

The only three restaurants worth considering groan with the same faces and food and people in limbo. How can I live rather than exist in this country? How can I hope to return as a reformed Hashem, guided by reason rather than by emotions? How can that be, when the only people I meet here endlessly say the one French word over and over, "Bon! Bon!," eat *kibbé*, accumulate wealth and money? Where are the books? Where is the air to breathe? Where is the continuity? Where are all those details which enrich experience? There is only this mass of people who listen, don't reply and think of nothing except an illusory tomorrow and the wings that will fly them back to Lebanon.

I have tried not to despair, but this African city is filled with clamor, din and people, with cards and players, all mixed up with the voices of drunken Africans in their cane huts. They made me responsible for the party in exile, but it was hardly a position for one who was a natural rebel. On the whole, the members didn't seek to debate or explore. Their loyalty to the party was more as if they had simply joined a new club. The feeling of being in limbo paralyzed their minds. The one question was whether our meetings here could ever become like those we had held in Beirut. I would nod my head as I looked at their protruding paunches and wondered at their questions and their faces grown shiny from constant exposure to the flaming mass of the sun. Meanwhile, news from home remained the same: every method, whether old or new, was being used to beat, torture, investigate. The régime which had been falling apart, that we had been poised to overthrow, was all at once solid again in its base.

While I remained an outlaw, a wanted man, a conspirator, the others came here to make a living. After a year here, they have made a fortune. After a few more years, they have become property owners and developers. They could buy up half the blue sea if they wished. The ornamental chairs in their houses irritate me. Their food irritates me. Always they use the one French word, "*Bon!*" and the habit weighs heavily on me. For them there is only one obsession: to collect a pile of money as they eat *kibbé* and play cards. Even my comrades in the party belong to the "*Bon! Bon!*" set of money makers and *kibbé* eaters. They have never tried to live in or discover Africa, as I once exhorted them to do at a party meeting. I asked why they never read books, why they did not follow current events at home or in the world, why they had only learned the one word "*Bon!*" and nothing more? In the end I threw them out.

The only one with whom I felt myself to be in sympathy was Majed. Our friendship grew stronger. I learned from him what it means to feel real hunger, the true reason for being an expatriate. He was from the south and had chosen to emigrate. As he said one day: "In the south I lived with flies and dust. I needed to get to Africa. At one time I believed it was made of diamonds, that they hung from the trees or were buried in the sand dunes, even as I believed that Saudi Arabia was strewn with gold watches." It shortly became clear to him that in Africa, as in Saudi Arabia and the rest of the world, it is necessary to work and toil before you can perceive, through veils of sweat and exhaustion, gold watches and diamonds.

I tried to persuade Majed that he should apply my theories about life in Africa to his dealings here, but his main thought by now concerned his getting married. He justified himself by saying that he didn't want an involvement with an African woman. He must have heard about my affairs with African women, since he made a point of telling me how he had denied such gossip about me. Instead, he had told people about my correspondence with Lebanon. I stared out of the window as I wondered what he was talking about. Which letters? Ah, the letters from my niece, Zahra. Those were the only ties I had with my homeland. Majed left me with my thoughts. My niece's letters were written on traditional Lebanese stationery.

Her letters were beautiful, despite being so sad. I doubted whether she actually remembered me, and I couldn't recall all that much about her. She must have been no more than ten years old when I left Lebanon. I asked her to send me a photograph of herself. I wanted to be clear about whom I was writing to. I couldn't think why she had started corresponding with me, in view of our age difference. I used to wonder, when I finished reading each letter, whether Zahra was aware that it was only through her writing that I maintained my links with both my family and my country.

What had become of friends, family and comrades? Years had gone by. There were no longer any dangers attached to writing to me. The Lebanese government had never ordered my extradition. The Ambassador and the Embassy staff were aware of my existence. I had written many letters home. To start with, my correspondents had replied enthusiastically, but gradually, one by one, they dropped away. Was it neglect or lack of affection? Or were they so self-satisfied that they could get by without writing? Did they ever read my letters through to the end? I doubted it.

The shortest letter I ever wrote home must have been at least ten pages long. It showed how disturbed I was. Perhaps Zahra felt the same, and that was why she wrote me page after page concerning various social problems. Sadness permeated her ambiguous sentences, written in their naïve style. She never wrote about herself, although I asked her to describe her life, to describe her average day in Beirut so I could hold those daily events in the palm of my hand and either regret or not regret being there.

Yet it was as if she never read my letters. She never responded to my requests. Always she wrote about the same subjects, and only once did she answer a question which I had put to her a year earlier. It was whether she would like to visit Africa. Her reply was phrased in one sentence: "My parents have agreed for me to travel to Africa." I had noticed how, of late, her short letters had begun to contain

passing references to death and despair and to these being
the source of the deepest happiness and peace which human
beings might attain. I tried asking her about those feelings,
about her problems, but she never responded. I wrote to her
brother Ahmad to suggest that Zahra needed to be cared
for, but he never replied.

My lofty position among my comrades, as they established their businesses and coffee factories, slowly eroded
until I found myself working as a simple accountant in one
of those same factories. My image as "Hashem the hero,"
who had made his escape through a hail of bullets after a
shoot-out with the military, remained. The halo was still
about my head, especially for the younger generation. But
gradually I grew accustomed to my existence. I stopped
troubling about delivering lectures. I stopped telling the expatriate Lebanese how to lead their lives. I became indiffer-
ent, especially after the correspondence stopped and I
learned there was no hope of my being able to return to
Lebanon for several years yet.

Sitting at gambling tables became a usual occupation. I
began to listen to this one or that one's stories and be enter-
tained by the details of their lives. I became one of those
eaters of *kibbé,* and even the word "*Bon!*" entered into my
everyday vocabulary.

It occurred to me how, when Zahra arrived in Africa, I
would be filled with sadness. She was my one remaining
link with my country. I anticipated that it would be a most
gentle sadness as my severed relations with my country came
to be momentarily renewed. Except for my name carved on
the trunk of a tree close to Saadeh's tree house, nothing of
me could remain there after all these years. My room could
never be the same, the sheets not smell the same. My school
books—I doubted whether they would have kept them.

Perhaps the weights I lifted were still behind the bathroom stove, but whatever remained of me there must, like the odors of cooking, have been swept away in a monotonous succession of days.

Now I was to receive news from home. I hoped that Zahra would know all about the fates of my comrades. I had asked her to find out in my last letter. It was my only request. "What do you want from Lebanon?" she asked. Of course, she expected me to reply "spinach pies," which are her mother's speciality and with which Fatmé was always trying to bribe me after she knew I had found out about her love affair with a man who was not her husband.

I never imagined that one day my feelings for Zahra would reach the pitch they did. I was only trying to express the strange condition which overtook me, once I had met her and let her sleep in my room as I slept on the living-room couch. After those long years, it seemed that I began to breathe again, and even to touch the fabric of my commitment to family and homeland. I felt I wanted to touch her hands and face and the hem of her dress. Through her I hoped to absorb all my life, both here and in Lebanon.

As I embraced her as tightly as I could, I thought how alike her face was to both her mother's and mine. She was a part of me. Here she was, after traveling thousands of miles, alighting in Africa like a tired, sad butterfly. I could never hear enough, and there was so much to tell. "Give me all the details," I demanded, "even if you think they're insignificant. I'm interested in every detail." There she was, lying in the next-door room, spread out on my own bed. I could hear her breathing. The house had previously felt so lonely as the air conditioner moaned on with the dust caught up in its works.

When I thought of all those invitations which I had had

to accept alone! Going to the beach alone, to the clubs
alone. Now Africa had changed. I would take her everywhere. I would buy her whatever she wanted. I would buy
her the gold bracelet that once caught my attention and
made me think how I should like to buy it for someone
dear to me, but I never found anyone worthy. When a person enters your life and changes everything, it is never
merely a question of coincidence.

The three restaurants, the thought of which made me
groan, seemed to brighten their images, their very tables.
The movie theater became more spacious. I felt that Zahra
was my key to making contact with my past and present as
well as my future. I thought that at last I could put down
roots in Africa, provided I had this witness of my own flesh,
blood and bones—a witness who could pick up the intensity of my glances, the beating of my heart, the trembling of
my hands against the huge tree trunks that resembled giants
and elephants. This tired, sad butterfly had alighted on me.
She didn't realize how I was like a new-hatched bird, opening its tiny beak almost to tearing point for one drop of
water, one grain of seed.

My sleep became disturbed and fitful as I agitated in my
bed, waiting. At day-break Zahra would still be in the adja-
cent bedroom, the sound of her breathing like a sign of
confidence and stability. I tried waking her, I sensed her
uneasiness. If I told her my feelings and held her shoulders,
she pulled away. If I simply used words without any touch
of my hand, she would remain as silent as the Sphinx, ignoring the ululation of the Egyptians and the pasha's horses
neighing. If I tried to wake her by leaning over her bed, she
would draw up the covers and transform herself into a block
of wood. If I persuaded her to dance, she would offer me a
hand of cold plastic. She was like that at the movies, too—

cold plastic. When I felt I could no longer repress my feelings, despite her silence and day-dreaming, she would turn on me: "What are you doing? What do you take me for?"

I am you, you are your mother, your mother is daughter to my mother. Let me hold you in my arms. Let me rest as your hand smooths my hair and you whisper to me: "Uncle, don't be afraid." The one act I ever effectively accomplished was to send you your ticket and then meet you at the airport. It makes me want to cry and laugh at the same time. You are the only witness to my destiny. Please don't reproach me and turn into wood. I can't communicate with a block of wood. I can't reveal to it my emotions. A block of wood has no living pores. It can absorb dew, but not my emotions, which are like streams that have swollen into torrents.

I tried to merge myself into the party, but never succeeded. My attempts stranded me here alone, despite the party comrades who shared my exile. Perhaps parties here cannot survive the humidity or the sun's ragged fireball. They become like no more than the breeze at the start of summer. If you were to turn into someone other than my niece, I would marry you. Don't whisper it to anyone. Your eyes have a sadness I like. In your silence there is a sadness I love. Don't whisper it to anyone. I am like a new-hatched bird waiting for one drop of water, one grain of seed.

Do you not realize that you are the only human being with whom I have had a relationship since the day I was born? As a child, I dreamt of playing with rubber tires. As an adolescent, my dreams became to run away from school and escape and hide in the darkness of a theater. After that, the party came into my life and sucked up my emotions, my nerves, my rebelliousness and coolness. With the party I finally established a relationship, but not with any of its members. In Africa it has been hard to establish any relationship, because everyone here is in transit. You are the only one with whom I have a relationship. I think such thoughts as, "What shall we eat? When will we go? What can we talk about? When shall we sleep?" and sit in my living room while a person occupies my bed and my room, a being who exists in relationship to me.

Can you grasp this, or do you use those pimples on your face to keep you busy, distract you from my words? You are family. A person without family is a lost soul. Why do you tremble? Why don't you let me cling to you and help me to forget this time in limbo? I will no longer sit and ruminate. My hope is reborn that I will return. I see your lips compressing. I see you pulling up the covers and backing against the wall as you ask, "What are you up to?" You say it after a long silence. Then you don't speak a further word and you go into the bathroom and remain there. You do not emerge!

4

H usband

I married Zahra without even knowing her. When I saw her and heard she was still a spinster, and that she was Hashem's niece, I thought: "Here is a ready-made bride waiting. By marrying her I'll be saved from having to go to Lebanon to look for a wife. I'll save the costs of travel and trousseau, for I've heard that brides here do not expect a trousseau as they do back home. Even if she insists, she wouldn't find shops like those in Souk Sursok. Even the jewelry here is different and less expensive."

I felt that I ought to get married, and lose no time about it, from the moment when I decided I would make in Africa a second homeland, even though there was no comparison between life here and life there. For the water in Lebanon is fresh, the light from the sky seems gentle, the mountains are beautiful, the climate has no equal. But none of this had been of any account when one strolled in the Bourj, able to afford to eat no more than a *falafel*. Poverty cancels out beauty in one's perceptions. I couldn't at that time visit Hamra, or the sea at Raouche, for those districts were reserved for another kind of person whose wealth made them alien to me to the extent where I was nervous of going to a cinema there, or strolling in the streets or even buying a cup of coffee. No doubt this nervousness stemmed from my earlier life, with few liras in my pocket, often only one. I feared that sense of being displaced.

Yet the important thing now was that I had managed to reach Africa after a good deal of effort. No sooner had my feet touched African soil than I began to get letters from friends back home, from the young in my village and even from some in neighboring villages, asking me to help them to emigrate. They would word their appeals: "Here, in Lebanon, no one gives a damn for you. If all you have is a piastre, then that is all you are worth." As I read those letters I would nod in agreement and think: "You're telling me. I know it only too well."

My earliest memories are of my father carrying his anvil, his hammer and a box of nails; of my mother preparing yogurt; and of flies on the noses and sore spots of my younger brothers and sisters. And then there was my stamp collection, which I used to think would bring me a fortune, and newspaper clippings and a few books. Everything I possessed was kept in the cupboard among the plates.

My emigration to Africa pleased my father so much that he would address his letters to me as if they were written to God rather than to his son. At the start he would evoke the name of God, the Merciful, and continue to go on thanking him till the end for the fact that I lived in Africa, like a human being and not an animal. And then, again, he would thank God for my good fortune.

But I needed to marry and beget children and to live in a

house like everyone else if I was to become a real human being. I needed to get rid of the shyness and sense of inferiority which had dogged me since the beginning. I needed to work constantly so as to stack money aside so that I could walk, proud and relaxed, in any place on earth.

There was one particular incident, or maybe two, which made me realize that I urgently needed to amass some money. The first occurred as we stood on the steps of the huge and only hotel here, waiting to enter the main hall to celebrate Lebanese Independence Day with the expatriate Lebanese community. We had heard about the celebration from a Lebanese who had been invited personally, and so we thought that the Embassy might not be able to trace us all. Yet, from the start, it seemed to me and my friends that no one here wished to know us. The rich Lebanese rolled up in their big cars, and no sooner did they reach the steps than Embassy staff rushed to kowtow to them and welcome them. As we stood, awaiting our turn, their eyes ignored us. Or, if they spared us a glance, they didn't stretch out a hand with the words, "You are most welcome," as we heard them say to the others.

Well, I told myself, they can't yet have spotted us, and I added, consolingly, that they must have been friends with the rich ones before. Then I went in and greeted them, and as they answered, they looked surprised, as if not expecting any ordinary Lebanese. My friends followed me hesitantly, and we found ourselves squashed together like a bunch of grapes or pickles in a jar. There was no celebration of Independence Day, nobody stood on a chair to give a speech. Instead, glasses of fruit juice and alcohol were passed around, and I didn't dare to touch one for the shining of the silver tray. It seemed as if these others didn't suffer from the

climate and the heat. It was as though they somehow
eclipsed the sun. One of the onlookers said how they even
had air conditioning in their cars and bathrooms.

I felt downcast and full of resentment. Then I asked myself why did I need to let myself get into such a state about
it all. I remembered the blond, stout man who had stood in
my cousin's shop one day in front of a transistor set which
he was thinking of buying. He addressed me in French. The
only French I knew was *"Banjour. Bansoir. Je vous zaimes."*
When I automatically muttered in Arabic, to my surprise
the blond man started to reply in the same. I was so thrilled
that I held out my hand to shake his and then crossed my
arm on my chest, as we do in the village, saying: "Greetings, cousin, to one who's surely a Lebanese. *Ahlan wa
sahlan."*

I didn't at first notice how the Lebanese "cousin" failed
to share my feelings as he stood nervously looking at the
transistor before putting his hand into his pocket to pay.
Meanwhile I went on asking him: "Would you like a drink?
Some coffee perhaps, or *gazouza?* Consider our shop as your
own. Please feel at home. I arrived only a few days ago after
many fights to obtain a visa . . . I rent a small room from
my cousin Muhammed. Please come and visit me. Do you
know Muhammed's house beside the Pepsi-Cola factory?"

But the man reached the door and left without a word.

My cousin Muhammed bore down on me in a mixture of
rage and laughter: "What came over you, Majed, son of
Salima? To whom did you imagine you were talking? To W.
Suleiman, no less? And you have invited W. Suleiman to
visit you?"

I felt embarrassed and perplexed, but responded, trying to
defend myself: "A Lebanese met another in Africa. What
should I do but greet him and invite him?"

But Muhammed didn't stop laughing, nor did the Africans in his shop. He wouldn't tell me who W. Suleiman was, but left me to find out for myself in time. W. Suleiman was a Lebanese judge who came from an aristocratic, influential family, but who had taken refuge in Africa for political reasons. I had thought that the fact of being far from home brought people closer together. How mistaken I was. It is only money which makes you strong in the world, gives a choice of friendships and achieves equality.

This is why I work so hard: so as to shower myself and my mother with money. Then I will forbid her to work any longer as a cleaning woman in Beirut, and together we will forget the past. When I accompanied her to work, she used to make me sit in the kitchen surrounded by pairs of shoes. Her excuse to her employer was that I was a shoeshine boy and that I had left my kit at the village since it was too heavy to carry. She used to lie, for I was sometimes in school, sometimes with my father, helping him carry his anvil and thick bundle of leather as he went around the villages. I would hear him say amid the sweat and stones: "Walk, my son, walk," and then we would call out together: "Shoe repairs, shoe repairs!"

I would sit in front of the shining shoes as if facing a clutch of difficult exam questions, for I used to be afraid of damaging the shoes instead of making them shine more brightly. I would curse my mother in a voice loud enough to reach the mistress of the house, hoping that then I wouldn't have to come next time, although I knew very well that she would make me. Having me with her increased the liras they paid her.

After a while I stopped objecting to my mother's insistence on me going with her, because the redeemer of my childhood left, and was lost to me: the donkey I used to call

"Safuan," the donkey I grew up with . . . the image of his bloodied hoofs . . . the donkey I loved and who loved me, who even recognized my name. They sold him. I had no idea why, and I ran after him and his buyer, who spoke to him in a harsh voice, "Hish, donkey!"

I cried out, with tears in my eyes, "His name is Safuan, not Hish!" I ran up to the donkey and flung my arms about his neck. But despite his love for me, the donkey left with his buyer, his bloodied hoofs stumbling on the rocks. He did not turn back. I ran after him, crying, "Safuan! Safuan!" I ran until I caught up with him again at the next village, where he continued to walk on without looking round.

I did not give up hope, but the buyer became irritated with my grief and pursuit. He turned and threatened me: "If you don't go away, I'll kidnap you and sell you to the gypsies."

I paid no attention. I kept on weeping and calling out to Safuan. My feet became as bloodied as his, and I only stopped running when the man turned in his tracks and held up the stick with which he was prodding Safuan into movement. He threatened me with the gold glint of his teeth, his thick eyebrows looking as if they belonged to Satan himself. He continued to threaten to kidnap me. Yet still I cried out, "Safuan! Safuan!" But the donkey never looked back. He left me as I went on repeating the same words: "Do you love me more than you love rice?" In this I was imitating my mother, who would often say to me: "Ya-Majed, do you love me more than you love rice?"

In Africa I sewed money-belts of white cotton in which to cache my money behind the refrigerator. My consuming obsession was to fill each belt with money; to fill a belt, then sew a fresh one. Once I realized that filling each belt was taking all my time, I finished serving in my cousin's shop and began to work in the store which Tallal owned.

Tallal would keep his store closed in the mornings, never opening up until after noon. He was not like us in his thoughts or habits. He lived for a day at a time, as he himself would say, and Africa was no land of lost promise for him, but a country like any other. He set out to enjoy every moment of his life, and therefore spent his time in the night-clubs, starting from nine in the evening, dividing his energies between women and the gambling tables. During the day, he would either be lounging at the seaside or asleep in bed. He had tried to open his store in the mornings by bringing in someone else to mind it for him, but he soon discovered that in this way he only lost a lot of money and business fell off.

When I was introduced to Tallal, he told me at once that he would like me to mind the store for him in the evenings, and so it came about that I did. Even from the beginning, he would rarely join me to sit with me, though I liked it when he did, for he was always good company. He relieved my heart of its aches. His absurd stories made me laugh. He had a way of mixing jocular and serious matters to the extent where his narrow eyes would grow more narrow and almost disappear under his forehead. He had thin eyebrows, and his smile never left his face, whether he was quiet or animated.

The strangest foods I ever tasted appeared on Tallal's table. He loved to cook for himself, and whenever he heard me say that I missed my mother's cooking, or *kibbé* with tomatoes, he would say: "Forget about *firaké* and *kibbé*! Are they better than lobster? Is there anything nicer than *paté* or caviar? Is there anything more delicious than avocado?"

At first I thought that he must be inventing these terms, because I hadn't learned to discern in the secret of his constant smile whether he joked or was serious. But when, one day, he took me along with him to buy the groceries, I realized that he had been using the real names of real foods. As he picked out mangoes, and papayas that were small and yellow, he told the story of his cousin who, the moment he arrived in Africa from Lebanon, asked to see the rubber trees which bore tires for fruit.

I began to feel tired, as I grew more sexually frustrated and continued to sleep with myself. Ever since I had arrived, I had not touched a woman. I had not been to bed with a woman since the one I used to visit in Beirut, who was over forty and kept a house in the Bourj red-light district. I can count the times, no more than ten, that I went to that woman's house. Whenever I have felt aroused, here or in Lebanon, it has seemed as if the scent of *falafel* and *tahini* suddenly fills the air. The woman lived above a restaurant, close to a bakery, and while I waited to receive the wink, I would enjoy the scent of *falafel* and have the urge to slip down for a minute and snatch a sandwich before it was my turn.

At that point I would wonder how much I really wanted to make love. A *falafel* seemed like a forbidden fruit. I would sit and imagine its taste on my tongue, but no sooner did my turn come and the woman tip me the wink than the smell dissipated and all my sensations came to be concentrated in the lower part of my body.

When I lived in the village, a special relationship existed between me and my body. I would close the door that had no lock and place a chair against it before I opened my copy of *Jane Eyre* in an Arabic edition and turned the pages till I came to the picture of the young heroine and Mr. Rochester kissing. At this point I would start to grow aroused and begin to seek to quieten that arousement quickly and nervously as my eyes furtively darted from window to door, from ceiling to picture. When I think of that small picture which stimulated me so effectively, it certainly makes me wonder. You would not have thought it was a picture that could possibly excite anyone's imagination, so innocent and commonplace did it appear to be.

At the time when I entered my world of secret masturbation I had no need of an outside stimulus. Everything was there, ready to fire within me, but after some years I felt that a routine had set in and was getting between me and my body and that I needed something more to promote excitement. Yet all I could find was the picture of Jane Eyre.

Then, however, I began to read in the magazine *Your Doctor* the advice being offered to the younger generation, which warned them to avoid this secret vice which could affect their minds. I tried to diminish my habit. One day my mother entered, after pushing open the door, and stood there in the middle of the room, balancing on her head a wide steel pan, not knowing what to make of my surprise and my hand in its embarrassing position. While she lifted the vessel from her head and bent her knees to place it on the floor, I seized my chance to pull up my trousers and dash from the room as she tried to detain me with her cries: "Woe betide you, Majed! How could you let the devil whisper in your ear? You're ruining your health and losing such a lot of weight. They'll take you away to Bihaness. You'll get tuberculosis, my darling. You'll never father children! Surely it's sinful not to be able to sire children. You should curse the devil the next time he whispers to you!"

My greatest fear was that, when I eventually married, my wife would discover my secret. She would be bound to leave me then, especially once the doctor had told her the real reason why I could not get her with child. When I was eighteen, I thought it would be a good idea to marry for the sake of sex, but none of the daughters of good families in our village would have me. It was their ambition to marry men who had either emigrated to Africa or who came from the city. I was told, before I left Lebanon, that Africa was a land of opportunity. I was also told that African girls would lie in wait for young white men as though they were birds to be hunted. My mother, too, must have heard that this was so. As she packed my clothes, she kept on saying, "Take care, Majed, take care, my love. Avoid those African girls like the plague. They have their ways of entangling white people, and as soon as a man succumbs, they get themselves pregnant. They'll stick like leeches and refuse an abortion. Once a child is born it will be yours, whether you like it or not. That's no problem if it's your own flesh and blood, but she probably slept with someone else five minutes before she came to you. You know Maha, the daughter of Derwish? She's the daughter of an African woman. You see how the other children laugh at her and say, 'Blacky-black with white teeth.' She has no future. Who would ever marry her, with that kinky hair and her rusty color? Poor girl! Do you want to have children who are persecuted like that, and you along with them?"

It was not her words, though, which stood between me and the daughters of Africa. It was their looks. I could never imagine my body uniting with one of theirs. I could never accept their thick lips, their barbaric hair, their black skin.

How I wished, when I first lay on Zahra, that she might scream and pound my chest and cry out, "Stop! Stop! You're hurting me. Please don't hurt me." But she only turned away her face, her body still under me. Even so, despite the fact that Zahra is not beautiful, I was so happy on my wedding night that I couldn't describe my joy. Here I was, married at last, the owner of a woman's body that I could make love to whenever I wished. From now on, surely my feelings of deprivation must dwindle: I have married Hashem's niece and so fulfilled the dream I've had ever since being in the south . . . of marrying the daughter of an illustrious family.

Even though our engagement had only lasted a week, it had been time enough for Zahra's family to reply to Hashem's cable. But I had noticed how she was not happy. She would stay quiet most of the time, and when she opened her mouth would be, by turns, aggressive or shy. The moment I put my arms around her, she would shy away and bend forward to avoid them. If I unshelled some pistachio nuts, she would take them but not eat them, because, she said, she did not care for pistachio nuts. When I took her to the restaurant with Tallal and his friends, I noticed she seemed happy, spoke quite a bit and smiled a lot, but she always refused to dance with me or Tallal. Yet I did not mind that she said no, since I never knew how to dance, anyway.

I was happy that I was married to her. Her changing moods had never stopped me or made me alter my mind about us marrying. It was normal for a woman to be moody at the outset. I felt sure that, as she grew used to me, so things would change.

On our wedding bed, she stretched out, avoiding my eyes. I felt her annoyance. This was as it should be. Girls are always irritable on their wedding night: fear and pain commingle. I felt she was in a state of disgust. That was also to be expected. It was her wedding night, and here was I, penetrating her. But, as she still avoided meeting my eyes, I

heard no cry of pain. Here was I, making love to her, me
the husband, she the wife. And there was no sense of a
barrier to my penetration. I saw nothing; the sheets remained white. Not even one drop of blood. Abruptly I
thrust her aside as she still avoided my eyes. I did not ask for
a sea of blood, I would have settled for one drop, but could
only cry out, as if in a trance, "Cursed woman! Daughter of
a cursed woman!"

She said nothing, but pulled the blanket about herself. I
dragged it off her and stared intently at her nightgown.
Nothing. Not a single drop of blood. When she tried to
cover herself again, I stopped her and cried out, "Have you
been married before?" She shook her head. "This is impossible! You are not a virgin." She answered nothing, and in
my pain I kept on and on persistently, "So you have illicitly
slept with another man before our marriage?" She still answered nothing, and for the first time it was of no account
to me that she was Hashem's niece. I shouted, "Tell me the
truth! Otherwise we go to Hashem together to get to the
bottom of all this."

Then she cried out fiercely that she knew nothing about
what I was saying, that she had been a virgin until I married
her tonight. Rejecting her stupid lies, I cried out, "Do you
take me for a halfwit? Just because you are Hashem's niece,
do you think I have to believe you and accept your claims
without question or conviction? Oh, no! If that is what you
think you are sadly mistaken!"

But, for hours, she only stared out of the window in her
stupor. I saw her face flush, her eyes become fixed. She
stared out of the window for one hour, two, three . . .
never speaking a word, neither eating nor drinking. She sat
there in her nightgown, mute before my questioning. The
blanket stayed in place, everything remained in place, except

for me. Eventually, in despair, I ran to the door, but heard her say as I did so: "Please ask the doctor to come. Let him examine me. He will tell you that I was a virgin when you married me."

I felt better once I had heard her say that, and told her, "My doctor does not pay house calls unless it's an emergency. Get your clothes on. We'll go and see him."

She stood up and shut the door on me, leaving me outside, thinking first one thing then another. The thoughts raced through my head, made my heart beat, made me knock on the door. To my surprise, she opened it and came out fully dressed. She left the house in front of me. It was some distance to drive to the clinic, and she sat next to me in the truck, her face pale, and swollen about the eyes. When I stopped the truck and opened the door for her to get out, she seemed unable to move by herself. I held out a hand to assist her. She walked in front of me until I moved up to her side.

The morning clinic was already full of Africans. I guided her by the hand, searching for two free chairs. Periodically the doctor opened his surgery door and peered into the waiting room. Each time he did it, I felt as if Zahra was on the verge of telling me something, but each time she hesitated and sank back into her stupor. As soon as the last woman had gone in and we were alone, Zahra suddenly told me how a man had raped her on her way home from work. I sat there fuming, mopping the perspiration on my brow. I sensed that the story was a fabrication. "Very good. So a man forced you to make love with him. What about the police? What about your family?"

The moment I mentioned her family, the thought occurred to me that perhaps they did know and had made a fool of me. Perhaps they had even sent her to Africa with the idea that she might make an idiot of some man there. Perhaps even her Uncle Hashem knew the truth and had duped me from the beginning. I was still turning all this over when the doctor looked in and nodded. But Zahra must have realized that my reluctance to leave the moment she made her confession showed I remained unconvinced by her story. Suddenly she gabbled out how she had been pregnant twice and undergone two abortions. I stood up and swept out. She followed. I got into the truck. I sat behind the wheel, trying to take in what she had said as Zahra struggled to open the other door. I had no desire to help her. I felt I hated her. When, finally, I opened the door, I noticed how she sat squirming in the seat.

I drove fast, glancing sideways at her as we went, seeing her swollen face and puffy eyes. I thought of my mother, of the alleys of the Bourj, of the smell of *falafel*. I thought how Zahra was now transformed from being a quiet, modest girl into an abominable, scheming woman. I thanked God that my mother was far away, far from this mess, and could not ask to see the stained sheets so that she might display them to Zahra's mother, to the neighbors and relatives. I thanked God for my mother's absence, and with it her stinging tongue . . .

When I was ten, early one morning, directly after my sister had been married to her maternal cousin, my mother sat and sipped coffee with her sister. As she sat, she wondered aloud why my aunt had not asked to see that piece of material. And my aunt answered, saying, "Oh, Um-Majed, it is a matter of no importance. Are we not sisters?"

In the same way, I now thought, Zahra's story could be my secret, for no one except myself had any knowledge of the truth. It comforted me, until I remembered that there had been another man. Who could this criminal be? Was it possible that people exist who can be so callous?

Zahra had meanwhile locked herself in the bedroom. She wouldn't open, despite my pleading. When, at last, she unlocked the door and let me in, I saw she had been sitting on the bed holding notepaper and pencil. I stood there as I asked about him: his name, his work, whether he really wanted to marry her and how I could help. She only needed to mention his name. Perhaps I could contact him and persuade him to marry her. Yet, as soon as I said that, it was as if I had touched the most sensitive nerve in her brain. She began to weep and shake, and curled up as if she were retreating into a shell. Then she dried her tears. She became, in an instant, a totally different person from the one who, a moment before, had wept and shuddered.

She stared into a void, stopped eating and drinking. My suspicions that Hashem might have played a part in the conspiracy dropped away when Zahra, in a state of hysteria, said that, whatever happened, she did not want her uncle to know. She knelt down, almost kissing my shoes, as if she were a character in a film or a story, asking for my forgiveness. "I beg you, beg you. Do not tell Hashem or my family. Divorce me and I will go to another country and find work. You won't need to be responsible for me. Kill me . . . do whatever you wish . . . but I beg you not to tell Hashem or my family. I beg you."

When night came, I felt worn down by it all as well as enraged and at a loss for what to do next. I felt I wanted to go to bed with her. I couldn't think why it was that this feeling kept growing and pressing upon me. But there she was, in the next room, curled up on the bed; there she was, demanding forgiveness. I went in, closed the shutters, turned off the light. I drew close and began to make love to her, not knowing whether she would turn her face away. An hour went by and she was still as rigid as wood. At times her eyes would be open, at others her face seemed expressionless. It did not trouble me. She was still scared, I thought to myself, but then (that word "but," it seemed, needed to be included in every thought and action) why had she accepted me in marriage if she had been so frightened at not being a virgin? Why had she married me? Did she think I would never realize the truth? Did I appear to be that stupid?

I slept fitfully with my painful thoughts. After several days, the intensity of these issues seemed to fade, as if such formidable questions become insignificant here in Africa, where there is no culture, no environment, no family to blow them up out of all proportion; for here every man stands on his own like a lone tree, like someone without a past who only has himself. Perhaps it is because there are no parents here, or because those who happen to be here have integrated into Africa and lack any culture to relate to. Traditions surface from time to time, but remain transplanted and so lose their former authority. My mother is either in the village or else in Beirut, working in somebody's house.

There is no reason why my mind should continue to be so troubled. Perhaps I should forget this whole business and start from scratch with Zahra, so long as she, too, can forget her past and grow happier, speak to me, help me with my work, bear my children. Perhaps we may even return to Lebanon as millionaires from Africa. But Zahra remains unyieldingly distant and cold, her eyes staring unblinking out of the window. She doesn't speak, nor does she move, except to visit the bathroom. I never see her eat or drink.

As days go by she sits on the couch with a transistor radio and a blanket as if she had leased this spot to be her new home and declared territorial limits.

I had no idea she was in such a bad way. I thought it was only because she was still afraid and ashamed that she pretended not to see me. The day came when I decided to tell Hashem of how she was behaving, and as soon as I told him he grew upset and confused. Without even waiting for me, he got into his car and drove to the house. He stood on the steps, banging at the door, ringing the bell. By the time I went up to open the door I was in a similarly enraged state. For a moment I thought, as he did, that Zahra had killed herself. I expected to find her body enveloped in flames. But there she was, glued to the window and to the radio which emitted Arabic songs.

The moment she saw her uncle, she looked at me, wondering what I could have said to him. To avoid further confusion, I told Hashem that I had no idea what the matter was with her. As he carried her out in his arms, I followed, taking the car keys and helping him to settle her on to the back seat. I started the engine, as he asked me to, while he sat next to her in the back. I drove to the hospital, as he instructed me, but could see no reason for taking this decision. What was this woman, except a liar, frightened of her own shame and making a pretense out of her remorse and regret? I could not see what connection a hospital would have with these self-evident facts.

I had no idea that I would, for a whole week, be taking the same route to the hospital to find Zahra in bed, her hair combed and a broad smile on her lips. That I would approach her and hold her hand and feel her response. That, at other times, I would find her with her face red and bruised.

It never occurred to me to wonder about her treatment since I considered I knew perfectly well what was wrong with her. Certainly there was no reason for me to intervene with her uncle paying all expenses.

Nevertheless, I had never before heard that hospitals could be for those who wept and those who quieted them down. My understanding was that hospitals existed to treat people who suffered from terrible diseases or needed operations. But why should I worry when Hashem was paying the bills? Zahra was suffering from a minor shock, he told me, at being separated from her family, and for this she was undergoing treatment. It made me laugh up my sleeve. I never tried to tell Hashem the true reason for her disturbance as I saw it.

When the day came for her discharge from hospital, I fretted over what I was going to say to those who asked after Zahra, for I was nervous of scandal. My initial concern was to keep her secret in my own interests, my feelings for her coming only second, but my biggest worry was what would now become of us both. I found I was irritated by her behavior as the reason and hope for which I had married her began slowly to erode. She had no fondness for me, would be no help to me in making a fortune from my work. It was clear that, in her present state, she would be incapable of looking after children. It seemed as if our roles had been reversed. Here was I, needing to take care of her all the time as she lay there, sometimes sleeping, sometimes staring like a madwoman who was trying to break out of the bonds of her insanity.

The day following her discharge, Tallal and his girl-friend visited us and brought some flowers. When Zahra ran to take the flowers, she merely shook her head instead of shaking their hands. She took one of the flowers and placed it in Tallal's lapel. She took another and threaded it into his girl-friend's hair. She stuck one in my shirt pocket and held yet another between her teeth as she began to laugh. Her laughter went on for a quarter of an hour. We all tried to laugh with her, but the attempt was false. Her movements were nervous, the expression on her face blank. She held the rest of the flowers and, walking to the wall, began to draw imaginary patterns. She stood there, drawing an invisible square and trying to place the flowers within it. The flowers fell to the ground, and again she tried to place them in the square, all the while cursing and insulting them as her face reddened. She turned and asked for some glue. In my embarrassment, I asked why she wanted it.

"Can't you see that I am trying to decorate my mother's picture with flowers?"

And I could not stop myself from crying out: "You cursed girl! In God's name, what a disaster you are!"

Tallal took me on one side into the kitchen and began to quiet me down. He said he would try to help me to find a solution. As we went back into the living room, we discovered Zahra tugging at Tallal's girl-friend's hand, trying to get her to wear the gold bracelet which I gave her on our wedding day, and as Tallal's friend refused, so Zahra was telling her in Arabic: "It is a gift from me to you, a token of our friendship."

We stood there, Tallal and I, completely nonplussed. I went up to Zahra to get her away from Tallal's friend, but Zahra flung herself at the girl, saying: "I wish her to take this gift. Why does she refuse to accept it?"

The more I dragged at her, the tighter she held on to the girl's hand and screamed and shouted. At that point Tallal stepped in and took his friend's hand to guide her quickly towards the door. Zahra slipped out of my grip, yelling at Tallal, who shut the door in her face, "Why are you running away?" She pounded on the door to the rhythm of her words like a rampaging storm.

5

Zahra in Wedlock

No sooner do I open my eyes than I wish I could close them again. I feel as if salt water is flowing in the space that surrounds me. When I shut my eyes, I see my father's watch and his fingers trying to wind it. I see my mother with courgette heads covering her face to smooth her skin, and I see her using a sugar concoction as a depilatory, trying to remove hair from her legs. I see her dressed in her robe and walking out on to the kitchen balcony. I see my father returning his watch to his little pocket.

Dear God! The things that I feel whenever Majed comes close to me! Cold winds, cold, crowding me close with thousands of snails crawling closer, crawling across the mud as the winds blow ever more strongly, carrying the snails' foul odor which soaks into every pore. I wanted to live for myself. I wanted my body to be mine alone. I wanted the place on which I stood and the air surrounding me to be mine and no one else's.

How long must I go on with this pretense? I tried to be

nice to his friend, Tallal, and to Tallal's girl-friend. I tried to act the gay, happy woman. And what happened? I pounced on them with my flowers. That's what Majed said I did, and that's what they said and what the entire Lebanese community said. Any hope of my ever being accepted as one of them is over. I have tried to make myself into what is expected.

I began to laugh and found no response, except that Majed dragged me back inside as soon as we went out on to the balcony, saying, "You have to be insane to laugh as you do." And that Lebanese woman kept staring at me. I must have been laughing very loudly and quite a lot. When Majed dragged me inside, it occurred to me to bite his hand and then escape into the jungle, but I only bowed my head until my neck disappeared and I retreated into my shell and kept my peace.

After several weeks, Tallal and his girl-friend invited us to attend a concert at which a Lebanese singer was performing. On the morning of the concert, Majed took me shopping to find a dress suitable for the occasion. It was the first time I had been out of the house since getting back from hospital. From the moment we went outside, I became drenched in sweat as the steamy damp fogged up my sunglasses and perspiration began to drip from my palms and armpits and to trickle down my thighs. I knew that later on, once those hot vapors had evaporated and the sun had set, I would be left feeling faint. At such times I felt I was beginning to understand the real nature of this continent.

Sitting next to Majed in the truck, I wished I could sleep, but it was hard to sleep as the truck lurched down that bumpy road. My uneasiness with Majed kept me alert, too. We went from one store to the next, Majed all the while expecting me to choose a dress. But I was frightened to touch any dresses. I only looked at one or two, and for no particular reason pretended not to like them. It happened in a dozen stores, and I couldn't understand why I was acting in this way, nor why I had agreed beforehand to go into those stores, knowing I would choose nothing because nothing was all I could see. Majed must have felt just as lost. He stood about hesitantly, unable to suggest, unable to speak to me in front of the store assistants. He simply went on standing. Only once did he point to a dress and say he liked it. But it was a dress meant for an outsize woman.

We left each store feeling terribly uncomfortable in the humidity and heat. As we came to the last one, he left me at the door, having handed me some money which I did not even bother to count. He said, "Buy whatever you want. I'll come and fetch you later."

As soon as he left me it occurred to me that now I could choose anything I liked. I saw a silver skirt, similar to one which Tallal's girl-friend wore. It had a matching blouse. Without a word, the sales woman showed me to a cubicle where I tried it on, stripping in front of the mirror on the wall. I must have been rather a long time about it, because the sales woman came in anxiously and asked whether anything was wrong. Seeing me still wearing the skirt and blouse, she asked whether I wished to buy them. I nodded; then waited for Majed's return.

As soon as I had put on my new clothes that evening, I went straight into the living room, where Tallal and his girl-friend were waiting. At once I felt their stares, and knew they were hardly stares of admiration. I sat and tried to make conversation, but I felt how their eyes avoided mine. I heard Majed heave a sigh. All at once he stood up and said, "Let's go."

At that instant I felt an enormous hatred for Tallal and his girl. Majed was constantly hanging on Tallal's approval for everything he did. Now I sensed that he was ashamed of me, and in the car became sure of it. The first thing Majed asked was how had I come to buy what I was wearing? Had I, indeed, even looked in the mirror? He handed me a tissue, told me to wipe my lipstick.

"You look like a cat that has just eaten its own kittens," he said. "How is it possible for anyone to wear such a short, tight skirt? Who do you think you are, girl? Some sophisticated woman from France or England?" And when I didn't answer, he continued, "It would be all very nice if the short skirt showed a pretty figure. But look at you, look at all this make-up. Your face is no better than a Halloween mask."

As he continued to scold me, I kept thinking that now I had lost all hope. Even if I were to try to be nothing except myself and stop trying to act and speak like any normal woman who wears clothes and laughs, then he would still find fault with me, and so would they all. The tears began to trickle, and although I tried to stem them, they kept coming as I blamed God for denying me the gift of beauty and even a talent for taking care of my looks. I put my hand to my face, tracing the patterns of scars left by my pimples. I told Majed that I would like to go home. I felt that he had been hoping I would say something of the sort ever since the moment when I went into the living room, but that, in Tallal's presence, he had kept silent as he fumed inwardly.

He leaned towards Tallal and conveyed my wishes, and there was no sign of a protest. Tallal swung the car about and brought us back. As he approached the wide street where we lived, he stopped to reverse on an unsurfaced sand track which I had never noticed before, along which there were several huts of sugar cane which served as cafés for the Africans, and, at the end, a small house with whose outline

I was only too familiar, having studied it from the window during my silent mornings.

As I left the car, I tried to say something but couldn't. Majed followed me into our home, grasping my hand as he asked why I hadn't said good-bye to Tallal and his girlfriend. I didn't reply, but dashed straight to the bathroom and locked the door. I kept rocking my head, rocking it as I screamed inside it and tried to scream aloud as well, though my cries stuck in my throat for my voice had failed.

Knocks came on the door.

"Leave me alone! Alone! I want to sleep! Sleep! Sleep! I don't want anyone to judge me or anything I choose to do or not do."

If only I could sleep for ever on the floor of this bathroom, the only place here where I do not feel I am in Africa. Where I can lose myself and not know where I really am. It is better for me to adopt this bathroom as my universe, until the knocks on the door cease, until the voice stops—the voice that I recognize out of a thousand voices because it is the only voice in this house . . . the voice of the one supposedly my husband.

Leave me alone in this bathroom! It allows me to disappear in time and space; it cuts me off from all human relations. It shuts off my memory from the time when I worked in the factory where the workers themselves were like so many cigarette packets, all looking alike, all having the same voice, and only I was different, with my uneasiness, with my fear of seeing Malek waiting outside the factory in his car; and then returning home to the fear that my father might have heard of my relationship with Malek . . . to the fear of my mother having made herself an expert in how a woman behaves as she strips naked before men. And with the naps which I took in the afternoon there came a fear of the reappearance of my *Qarina,* the kinship spirit of which my grandfather spoke, a jinn who invades a person's body and lies low there until, no sooner is one on the verge of sleep, than it appears, especially during the day, and starts a struggle and sets off nightmares. When I was a girl, whenever my struggles began with my *Qarina,* I would be unable to open my eyes. I would try to shout and release myself with all my strength, but my vocal cords would be paralyzed. The *Qarina* stood between me and my sight, my voice, my thoughts. There was the time when I heard knocks on the door, on the floor, and anticipated every knock as it came, as if each knock was of deep significance. I tried to open my eyes, but couldn't; I tried to scream, but my voice froze. The knocks continued. I tried to scream, but there was no sound. At last I did open my eyes to see my Aunt Najiba standing on her wooden leg, in her hand a bundle of clothes, on her head a black scarf.

Finding me staring at her as if she had stepped down from a flying saucer, she said, "My, how you do sleep, little niece! I've been standing here for more than fifteen minutes and you still slept! It's a good thing I'm no thief, Zahra. Where is your mother?"

Yet I was still struggling with my *Qarina,* which seemed about to strangle me and not to be departing, as it usually did. So I told my aunt about my *Qarina.* She recited the opening verse of the Qur'an, and when she had finished, opened a bundle of cloth bags and made up tiny reticules of kishk, marjoram and other herbs.

I wish to remain for ever in this bathroom despite all the knocks on the door that still throb in my ears and the voice of the stranger who has entered my life because I was once spread out on the old doctor's table as his nurse combed her hair and casually put on lipstick. Because of that I am here, in this stranger's bathroom.

I never want to leave this bathroom. There is the voice of my Uncle Hashem, my close relative, that other stranger. I hear my voice fade out as if my *Qarina* has visited me in my waking hours and severed my vocal cords. Here I am, under siege in the bathroom, and my Uncle Hashem's voice asks me to offer one word of reassurance. Does he imagine I have killed myself?

When I opened the door and entered the living room, looking for a transistor radio and a bedsheet, I saw and heard Majed beating his head with his hands as he told my Uncle Hashem how he was at his wits' end.

"The day before yesterday they saw her walking round the outside of the house, carrying the radio, playing it turned up so loud that God himself could have heard it. Madame Zahra carrying a radio, dancing in the street. Yes, by heavens! Even gypsies would be ashamed to do such a thing!"

Encountering only my uncle's silence, Majed yelled out, "I can't stand her or her behavior! What have I done that God should punish me in this way? Help me, cousin, and let you and I remain good friends."

Where is my *Qarina*? Why doesn't she visit me any longer? Is it because I no longer take naps during the day? Or is it because sleep now comes to me in the day as easily as it does in the night and she no longer knows when I am awake or asleep? Is it true that she did once visit me during the day, and called on me, and that when I grew scared I would not answer her?

My Aunt Najiba would tell me that a *Qarina* is both good and evil. Everyone is accompanied by one from childhood,

and she will visit them without ever making herself visible.
Should any person doubt the existence of their *Qarina,* she
will let the one standing next to that person hear her voice
so that he believes in her and is convinced and so, in turn,
convinces the one to whom the *Qarina* belongs that his
name was called.

Once, when my mother took me south to visit her father, she left me in his tobacco booth as her man waited for
her, somewhere out in the fields. Time moved slowly, despite my being with my grandfather. He was concentrating
on piling the tobacco leaves in front of him and he stayed
unusually silent. He did not even stop to take out of his
pocket some piastres so that I might go and buy a few nuts
and sweets. He was anxious to get through his work
quickly. The trade association to which he belonged, named
the "Sons of the South," was due to gather to elect a dele-
gation to send for a meeting with their parliamentary dep-
uty.

I was at a loose end. I tried to work with the tobacco.
The work was much harder than I expected and was made
harder by the sun beating down on the booth's corrugated-
iron roof. Heat rose from the floor and the water in the
pitcher was lukewarm. I left the booth to explore the alleys.
The houses seemed like mirages, uninhabited, their colors
faded. Under the sun's glare, the scene resembled an ancient
citadel with a small mosque and rows of houses, stairways
and alleys. I undid my black shiny belt and dragged it behind me as if it were a donkey until I came close to a large
pond in which were frogs, dirt and discarded debris. Everything was quiet. I looked around and asked, "God, send me
a companion to play with." I dipped my belt into the water
and leaned over the pond, and suddenly saw in the pond the
image of a girl. I was not dreaming. I stared intently at the

reflection, and it certainly wasn't me. She had no ribbon in her hair, as I did. The hand holding the belt was a different hand in the pond. The shape of the face was different. And I heard my name being spoken, as if someone whispered it, as if the lips of the girl in the pond moved. Frightened, I turned back towards the booth, running, stumbling on the stones, falling and getting up and stumbling again. The distance between the pond and the tobacco booth seemed infinite and I thought, "When will I get there? When?" As I arrived, my breath was coming in gasps. I tried to control it. I tried to catch and quiet my breath, but when I couldn't I thought, "Perhaps this is the voice of the girl who just appeared to me." Frightened, I stood in the booth entrance, seeing the pond in my imagination. Yet never again did my *Qarina* show herself to me after that time when she called to me and scared me so badly.

"What is the solution?" Majed asked in a voice half-composed, half-hysterical.

I answered, "Let me go to Beirut for a while. Then I will come back."

And I began to cry. My uncle came up to me, touched my neck, and I cried even more because I couldn't pull away from his hand, because in this situation, in which I felt like a rat in a trap, I could do nothing except cry. I felt his cold hand and its beating pulse on my neck. Everything about my uncle seems to have a pulse-beat.

I raised my head to hear what Majed said, but it was my uncle who replied. He said he would make a flight reservation for me the next day. He asked whether I would care to spend the night at his place while arrangements were made for my departure. I shook my head, which pleased Majed, who said, "This is Zahra's home. If she wishes it, I will leave the house, I am quite prepared to do so."

The first thing I saw at Beirut airport was my father's frowning face, questioning what the matter was from the other side of the glass partition. I saw my mother's round face, seeming about to explode, so full was it with suppressed anxieties. I had forgotten what would await me in Beirut.

As soon as I was among them, my mother came up and I kissed her. My father, who barely let his face get close to mine, asked, "Zahra, tell me, why have you returned? It's only a month since you were married. What are we to say to people? What are we to tell Majed's family? I hope his affairs prosper and that is why you became his wife."

My mother could not restrain herself from asking eagerly, "Tell me, Zahra, is it true that his mother used to sell vegetables and came to Beirut to work as a cleaning woman?"

I did not know how to respond. I mumbled, "Once we get home we can discuss everything."

In the taxi, my mother leaned across and whispered, "Are you hiding something from us, Zahra?"

I answered, not thinking, "No, mama, what is there to hide?"

As if realizing that I had not understood her, she whispered in my ear, "Are you expecting? Are you pregnant? Is that why you have come?"

I smiled and shook my head. It was as if I had broken all the threads of her hope. My mother had thought I must be pregnant, never doubting for a moment that this must be the situation and the explanation. And so now she asked quickly, "But in that case, why have you come? Is there something between you and your husband? Have you quarreled? Every day of my life I have gone on wondering who in the world would ever marry you. You are like the Sphinx, never speaking a word or smiling."

I realized she hadn't asked about her brother. I thought of Majed and how upset he was. I thought, too, about Malek and wondered whether he knew of my marriage and of my returning to Lebanon. I did ask my mother about Ahmad, but my father's face showed concern and he put a finger to his lips, indicating that this was, for the moment, an inappropriate question.

Nevertheless, I whispered in my mother's ear, asking after Ahmad. She answered, "Ahmad, may God guide him, is very lost and confused. Later we'll tell you how things are."

She continued to stare at me, with many questions in her eyes, though her lips stayed silent. After some moments she continued, "What have you done to your face, Zahra?" She was gazing at my legs so could hardly see my pimples, but she went on, "What does your husband say when he looks at those pimples on your face? It seems you still can't stop yourself squeezing them till they burst."

All at once I realized to where and to whom I had escaped. I would never be able to convince them that the reason for my coming was because I had missed them. I felt helpless before the onslaught of my family's questions, as, before long, I felt helpless in the presence of Majed's family, who turned out to be peasants in every sense of the word. His mother would begin to cry every time his name was mentioned, while her face seemed constantly to ask whether or not he had sent her some money; and on receiving an answer, she would cry again and rock her head back and forth. The situation revealed the truth about Majed, which Africa had been able to conceal. His acceptance of all my problems and stories, of the fact of me being no longer a virgin, had puzzled me. But here was the background from which he came: from the womb of this thin woman, from the groin of this father who, with great difficulty, struggled to open his fair eyes, and sported a handkerchief on the side of his red fez. Did Majed then emerge from the womb of a mother who could not even utter normal speech?

I realized what an immense gulf existed between our family backgrounds and saw the answer to the mystery of why he had married me, despite all my shortcomings: my pimples, my constant clumsiness, my moodiness, the fact that I ignored so many social graces. This was why he had kept quiet after discovering all about both me and my nervous fits.

Once, when my parents were refraining from their usual persistent questioning over the reason for me coming back, I told them, as we sat round the kitchen table eating dinner, that I had had a nervous breakdown and been kept a week in hospital. I think that they had, by that point, given up all hope of getting any answers out of me, since I had gone silent every time they had asked me my reasons for returning home.

While I was still in Africa, I had never dreamed that I would be caught in such a trap. I never thought that asking for a divorce could be so difficult. It had all seemed so easy, sitting under the bed-covers on the couch and listening to the transistor. The great distance between the two continents had made me think that anything I asked of my family in Lebanon would be granted and that all I needed to do was leave Africa. But, from the moment when I saw my family's faces staring through the glass partition at the airport arrivals lounge, the assumption changed and the problem grew into one of enormous proportions.

The more I saw of them, the harder it became, and as I sat amid them and their conversations, I realized that it would never be possible for me to tell them the whole truth. And so the idea died out from my heart and mind.

Days passed, and I remained a prisoner in the house in Beirut. I never felt like paying visits and always pretended to be tired whenever my mother told me that someone or other would like to drop in to offer congratulations. Maybe I prompted my mother to react in the same way, for whenever the door bell rang she would have her answer prepared —about some mythical miscarriage, about how primitive medicine was in Africa.

I grew restless in my prison. My father still wore his uniform, although there were no longer any tramways in Beirut, and he still wound his watch, brought it to his ear, spoke in his habitual clipped phrases. He would leave each morning, come back each noon, carrying the same paper carrier bags and packages of food, bread, watermelon, cheese. My mother rarely left the house, and would hide her hair under a scarf and put on a black coat over her dress. She no longer seemed to be the woman with dancing blue eyes and blue silk dress who once used to run to Dr. Shawky's clinic and then on to her lover's room, the woman with whom I would climb rocks till we reached the walnut tree and who I wished would hold me in her arms for ever.

My Aunt Najiba told me long ago how my mother's man friend married after he despaired of her ever divorcing my father and after my aunt had threatened to kill him.

The idea of going back to Africa was not so strange to me by now, especially after Majed had sent me three letters, urging me to return and telling me how much he missed me. It seemed as if someone else must have written those letters. I could not think of a single reason why he should want me back. Why all this longing, when our relationship was nothing like a normal relationship between a man and a woman? I could not recall a moment in it when I had been happy, when I had not been silent and felt depressed as he made love to me or even merely came into the house. As the wife of his dreams, all I had brought him was deception and disappointment. Then his letters arrived from a world that was different at least from the world within the walls of my parents' house, from the world of my father's constant worries, from the world of my mother, who created memories only of the former mother with whom she had no connection, having become a *hajja,* a woman who has made the pilgrimage to Mecca; a worrying mother, concerned for her daughter's future after giving up hope of ever making a future for her son Ahmad.

I only saw Ahmad twice in all that time. He had first tried to be a merchant in the market place, and then had become a ticket tout for the movie houses before finally taking up work as a taxi driver.

I decided to return to Africa. There was no other way out. Whenever my mother prayed at dawn she would say a special prayer, asking God to return me to my husband. Whenever I met my father's eyes, he would ask the same question: "Zahra, should I reserve a seat on the plane for your return to Africa tomorrow?"

My life with them involved a constant interrogation at every turn, or so it seemed. I felt embarrassed whenever I reached out for a piece of bread or took a second helping. If I washed any of my clothes, I felt guilty at using a little detergent. My return had shown up a deep gulf between my family and me. I no longer belonged in this household. It was as if their duties towards me had ended with my marriage. My father still considered that my original reason for leaving for Africa had been to escape from marrying Ahmad's friend, Samir.

As I packed my bags I thought, "Why shouldn't I start a

new life with Majed? Why shouldn't I treat him as a friend and begin working with him, accepting his ideas and helping him to save money? I don't need to forget that I am capable of keeping my feelings to myself, especially since marriage, after a while, becomes a sort of contract. That was what Malek used to say. That is what everybody says. All I need to do is keep my real self hidden."

These simple solutions preoccupied me, so that whenever my thoughts of Africa came back as a nightmare, I would revert to my musings, seeing, from my return to Lebanon, the kind of life which I would lead, were I to stay as a prisoner in the house, a prisoner among my family and their intentions. Therefore I would return to my own home in Africa, where I could become anything I wished, despite my having taken up the role of wife on no more than a couple of occasions since my marriage.

The day that I arrived back in Africa it was raining. I saw Majed and my uncle from a distance, and saw they had seen me coming. I turned away for a moment, as if I didn't want to recognize them, but I was aware that they were drawing closer. Suddenly I felt like crying. I felt the trap snap shut again. I couldn't look Majed in the face, couldn't talk to him or listen to him, wouldn't be able to watch him eat. He was a stranger whom I hated. All of this had come flooding back, and we were still within the airport confines, still with my uncle amid the crowds of travelers. How, then, could I hope to be able to overcome such feelings for Majed once we were alone together?

Was this trap real? If so, how did I come to be returning at this moment, or thinking of remaining another second in Africa? It was raining, my heart was raining, my mind was raining, pouring out the thoughts that filled it, trying to reason, to arrive at some logical conclusion. But I had closed off every escape route and could only see myself caught in a net as sobs broke in my throat.

How could I have returned to Africa, after those skies had opened up to me and carried me back to Lebanon? How could I, so freely and willingly, have returned to this trap? None of those here could avoid it, not even the ones who set it. But my uncle was saying, "Blessed be God for your safe return, Zahra." He steered Majed closer as I stood, rooted to the ground. I held out a hand, greeted them. Majed's hand touched mine, and at once the cold snails began their slow trailings, enveloped in thin layers of perspiration as they crawled on to my fingers and hands, spreading all over my flesh. No! Enough! I was waiting for someone to save me. I could not save myself.

Might my uncle save me? He seemed my only hope. He had saved me the first time, but now things were taking their course. I could not divert their course. My uncle and Majed took my luggage, put it in the car, opened the door, got in, drove me homeward. We reached the house very quickly. It was already too late for me to ask my uncle to save me. He said he would drop by later to see how I was.

As soon as I was alone with Majed, I felt overcome by my hatred. He wiped out all the ideas about our starting a new life together which had filled my head. As he came up to me, I felt his breath and with it felt disgust. I looked away, but could only see the rain outside the windows.

I averted my face, but stayed calm. He asked about his family. I answered without looking up. He tried to put his arms round me. I slipped away. He drew close. I stepped back. He followed. I screamed, but he ignored my cries. I tried to push his hands away, but he was set on having a fight. I screamed again, hoping someone would hear, but we were alone except for the constantly falling rain.

I forced him away, making up my mind that he would never touch me unless I were dead, lifeless, as it had been with our foreign neighbor, a woman with a dog, when she defended herself to the death as the hair-dresser tried to rape her, and everything ended in seconds, except that her dog went on barking for days.

Majed remained insistent, and I went on defending myself until my resistance began to fail, my crying still having no effect. Then I bit his hand with all my strength and heard him bellow, "Damned woman! Bitch! Animal!" as though he had gone out of his mind. He tried to pull his hand away, but I was determined that after this he would do nothing but hate me. I fell on to the floor as he pushed and then kicked me. He threw me down on the couch as I went on ceaselessly screaming and moaning.

I shouted, "Divorce me! Divorce me!" and heard him say, "Get up and get dressed, you mad, mad woman. You are insane! Why did you return, cursed woman? Why? What do you want from me? A million girls would be happy to have me. You are crazy and off your head. Who do you think you are? Do you imagine you are something so grand? Go and take a look at yourself in the mirror and come back and tell me what you see there!" And the flow of his words went on: "God preserve us. I spit on you, niece of Hashem. Oh, we are indeed honored! Uncle Hashem may well be a famous person, the leader of the PPS and all that, but, I tell you, I'd rather be married to the niece of the refuse collector. Damn you, get up and put on your clothes! You should put on the clothes of the Angel of Death rather than your own. Damn you, get up and get your clothes on

before I tear the head off your body!" He brought his face
an inch away from mine as he shouted again, "Get up! Get
into your clothes!"

As soon as he realized I was fully dressed, he dragged me
out of the house and opened the door of the truck. I
climbed in with difficulty, still shaking with tears and trying
to hide my terror. Yet I felt that my deliverance was near,
that I could take anything except living under the same roof
as Majed. As we drew up outside my uncle's home, we saw
that his car was nowhere about. Majed turned the truck
around, and from then on I became truly petrified because,
each time that I convinced myself he had calmed down and
become more rational, the vehicle would suddenly swerve
and accelerate so fast that he seemed sure to turn it over.

Glancing sideways, I saw his pale face. I needed to clutch
on to my seat with both hands, he was going so fast. It was
as though he wanted me to be thrown out on to the road. I
had no idea where he was heading and couldn't ask. It occurred to me that he might be looking for somewhere to
dump me.

We came to an abrupt halt outside a small house, in front
of which I recognized Tallal's car. Majed got out without
saying a word, slamming the door in a way that spoke many
words. I sat on in my fear, but knew this could not last for
long. With my eyes fixed on the door, I waited for Majed
and Tallal to appear at any moment. But I sat on and on.
The rain went on falling. The heat and humidity were all
about me.

But by now I liked waiting. I would have been happy to
wait on my own for ever. The rain streamed down and the
heat saturated my head as I wondered, "Why is it that I am
always finding myself in a hurtful situation? Even doing no
more than lying in bed back in Beirut, there would always

be something which troubled me. Is a person born with this uneasiness, even as a person might be born with eyes of a certain shape, hair of a certain color? Ever since I can remember I have felt uneasy; I have never felt anything else."

What was keeping Majed and Tallal in the house? Tallal hated me from the first time we met. He was the first to put me in my place as a girl below average in personality and attractiveness, who had nothing to recommend her beyond the fact of being Hashem's niece.

When Majed reappeared and came back to the truck he was alone. I didn't know whether he was looking at me, or what the expression was on his face. As we drove down the road, I kept hoping that he was looking for somewhere else for me to stay until the time came for me to go back to Beirut. I clenched my fists, perspiring and hoping that he was not taking a route back to his house. Suddenly he turned and asked whether I wanted a divorce. I nodded.

"Say that in front of your Uncle Hashem, because I will not pay one penny in divorce settlement."

Feeling relieved, I asked, "Who is asking you to pay anything?"

He replied, "Even though you haven't thought about it, your family could well be counting on it."

I answered, "You're wrong. My family is not like that at all. They don't care about money. Their concern is for my happiness."

He turned to me with venom and yelled, "Your happiness? When have I ever hurt you?"

In this he spoke justly, and so I said nothing, but I might have replied, "Never mind. I don't think I am made for marriage, and once the divorce is through, I will have nothing to do with any man. I hate all men." But I could not open my mouth. I could not speak. I wanted only to sleep.

At my uncle's home, his car was parked outside by this
time. Majed indicated with a nod of his head that I should
get out. I stood to one side as he rang the bell once, twice,
three times before my uncle, with bloodshot eyes, narrow
lips and squat body, came to unlatch the door.

He greeted us with great surprise, gathering his bathrobe
about him. He seemed lost for words and suddenly realized
that he was still clutching the half-open door. When he
opened the door wide and let us in, Majed asked whether
we had woken him up. He replied, "That's of no conse-
quence. After all, here is Zahra and she's my niece. Don't
mention a thing."

I sat on the far end of the couch as Majed began to speak:
"With Zahra's permission, I have to make certain matters
clear."

And he began to recount everything that had happened
between us since the day of our marriage, my uncle remaining silent. But my uncle cleared his throat after Majed
stopped talking and, to my surprise, told Majed that the
question of whether or not I was a virgin was beside the
point and not worth mentioning. Educated people understood this well enough and would never dream of bringing
the matter up.

"It is all very easy for you to say such things, Hashem,"
Majed interrupted, "but . . ."

My uncle replied as he shook his head, "Believe me,
Majed, I never say anything which I don't believe. Perhaps
you don't know me well enough, but you can ask anyone.
This is not something to make a fuss about in the twentieth
century. Our generation should be seeking to influence our
parents and those whose minds and attitudes remain narrow.
But the thing which really concerns me in all this is Zahra's
future. Perhaps Zahra should have married this man about

whom you have told me. Maybe we ought to help her to marry him.'' Then my uncle turned to me and said, ''Come, Zahra, why do you stay silent? Is this the way to be married—to marry someone while your mind is preoccupied with someone else?''

I drew a deep breath and thought how out of touch he was, truly lost in Africa. Then my inquisition began. He asked his name, his work, why we hadn't been married if our relationship was so important. My response was to stare at the dish of fruit on the table. He resumed his questions, guessing at answers and saying, ''Perhaps he was a Christian and you were afraid of your father. Perhaps there's another reason. Why didn't you write to me about it? All those letters, and you never even mentioned him. What is the real story, Zahra? Come now, we'll solve this problem together. Come, my dear niece, who is this man? We'll help you to return to him. We want you to be happy.''

I thought how far off the track he was, and how much better it would be for him to drop the subject, for I would never open my mouth. I kept staring at the dish of fruit, and, hearing footsteps, turned to see an African woman in Western clothes, showing most of her breasts and with gold sandals on her feet and red lipstick on her lips. She entered the living room from my uncle's bedroom, as if she had been waiting for some sign from him, but he went on talking to me although he kept looking at her. She nodded a greeting to us, then went out of the house. As my uncle continued to speak, he stared fixedly at an astonished Majed, as if deliberately assuring him that, yes, there really had been an African woman, and yes, only a short while before he had been in bed with her.

Gradually his patience with me ebbed away as I never took my eyes off the fruit dish. His voice grew louder and more agitated. He insisted that he must know the man's name so that my family could contact him. He said he would himself contact him that very night, by telephone or cable. I asked myself what chance did I have of making him see things otherwise, of altering the picture he had built up and explaining the true nature of my relationship with Malek? How could I express it in simple terms and say that this was something which really had nothing to do with me —that, from beginning to end, I had been a mere spectator.

Oh, my uncle, if after all this, you were to ask me whether I loved him, I would have to tell you, "No, I never loved him. I couldn't stand him. But I was hypnotized. Maybe he possessed written charms or got witches to write them." Why did I always go to him, even though I had no feelings for him at all? How did my fear become so dominating? Why did I let that amazing fear take over every moment of my life, even when I was working in the factory, so that I would think of Malek waiting for me in his car, sitting outside the main entrance? Why did I let it consume me and, bit by bit, make me ravage my face till it looks as it does today?

I have lived in a cyclone of uncertainty and fear. I could so easily have thrown him out of my life. I only needed to say "no" once. Was it weakness that I did not do so? If so, what was its nature? Why did it pick on me? Why did Malek pick on me? Why did I remain only a witness and spectator? It is not, my uncle, because I am frightened of your scorn or anger or silence that I cannot tell you. I cannot tell you because I simply do not know.

I stopped staring at the fruit dish, looked up and said, "Perhaps we should try one more time."

Majed, startled by this fresh surprise I had sprung on him, stuttered unhappily as he tried to grasp what I meant. But then he turned about and said, "Yes, perhaps we should try just once more."

As for my uncle, he mumbled, totally baffled, "Surely, Zahra, you cannot be serious?"

But by now I was again convinced that I must accept the solution that came to me in Beirut, that I had to start afresh.

When we got back to the house, I told Majed we must get married again. He said that we were married already. I told him that I wanted to get married once more. I began thinking of whom to invite, of who would preside over the ceremony. Majed, totally astounded, kept staring at me. But he only said I ought to sleep after my long trip.

It was hard to believe that only that morning I had been in Beirut. It seemed that many years had passed since I arrived back in Africa, and that an infinity of rain and dampness had soaked into every object there, even the houses and cars. It seemed as if I had aged since that very morning. I expected to find a sprinkling of white hairs which I had never seen before when I went to the bathroom to get undressed. Deciding to wear a housecoat over my nightgown, I tip-toed off to bed.

I hoped to pretend that I had been asleep for a while before Majed came in from the balcony, where he was sipping arak, but he entered the bedroom only a few minutes behind me and, slipping into bed, turned his back on me. A few moments later I could hear him breathing steadily. He was actually asleep. Now I could sleep myself. I lay on the edge of the bed, drawing up my knees to my chest and hugging my arms about me. In the morning, when I awoke, I went into the bathroom to dress. It seemed that life could, in fact, be simple and beautiful, as it had been last night and was this morning.

For the first time since our marriage I began to prepare

breakfast. When Majed entered the kitchen, wearing his pajamas, I felt annoyed but didn't show it. I wanted him only as a friend and didn't like to see a friend wearing pajamas. He sat and ate breakfast in silence. This time it was I who started the conversation as I reminded him of our plans for the wedding celebration that evening. He continued to show bemusement and asked if I were truly serious. I nodded.

When evening came and his friends and their wives began to arrive, I noticed the strange expressions on their faces. I couldn't quite make out whether these were looks of pity or of astonishment. As the evening went on, their true nature gradually emerged: astonishment began to swamp pity. Each conversation started and ended in the style of: "How are you now? Much better, I hope. Let's pray to God there is no recurrence." They scrutinized every inch of me and no doubt laughed and whispered about me whenever my back was turned.

That evening I tried very hard to be one of them. Majed put on records and invited everyone to dance. With the living room crammed with men dancing with their wives, I found myself the only one still seated. I urged myself to stand up and dance, to banish my timidity there and then, so that I might become like the rest. Here was an evening of celebration for my decision to marry. This was why there was dancing and singing. All at once I found myself in the center of the room, my eyes closed, my body turning in circles and one foot moving in front of the other. I tried to wriggle my belly, but couldn't. I swayed my back and shoulders.

The music grew ever louder and faster. I went around and around, trying to keep my hands and feet, my belly and back moving in time. Then the music changed to African drum music—music, perhaps, of the very tribe of the man-servant who cleaned the house and who knew of my return.

Was this him coming to greet me with his drums and musical instruments? The music grew louder still and I swayed to left and right, just like a procession of mourners I had once glimpsed from my window in Beirut: women in white moving to the right and left, time after time after time. The music made me shake my head to its rhythm. The music changed again.

Suddenly I could stand it no longer. I had to stop, but couldn't. I must stop. The room was dizzying round. A voice said, "Have you had enough, Zahra?" After a time I let go of the arm on which I was leaning, but was aware of eyes staring at me. My uncle was gripping my arm as he tried to push me out of the room. The faces surrounding me criticized every move I made. Two of them were laughing at me, but trying to hide their mockery. I turned on them, screaming, "You are all pathetic animals! What are you laughing about? You were all dancing yourselves. Leave my house! Get out!"

My uncle intervened and led me into the bedroom where he made me lie down on the bed. I fell into a sleep so deep that I never even wondered where Majed would rest. When I awoke in the morning I felt so weak I could hardly stand. My uncle came into the room, saying nothing. He helped me to walk to the bathroom, where he waited until I was done, then brought me back to bed.

He sat on my bed and asked, "How do you feel, Zahra?"

I turned my head away. I had caught a quick glimpse of myself in the mirror on my way to the bathroom and seen my red and swollen face. After my uncle left the room,

Majed entered, practically whispering, "How are you today, Zahra?"

Once again I turned my head away and tried to bury my face in my hands. After a while, Majed left, and I looked at my hands and noted their blue, distended veins. I saw my fingers swollen and wrinkled and wanted to examine my feet, for I felt a pressing urge to rub them.

My uncle came back with the doctor who had treated me the time before. Without a word, he held my arm and injected me with a syringe. He half-smiled as he left the room. My uncle sat down again on the edge of the bed, and I was aware that he asked, "Would you like to leave for Beirut in a couple of days?" But the prospect didn't impress me. It was all the same to me: going to Beirut or staying here to watch from my bed as the rain fell outside the window. It made no difference to me. I would like everything about me to grind to a halt and for me to become like a window through which one looks and through which things are seen to move, while the window itself remains silent and still, observing people come and go. Now I would have liked to sleep, although I could hear Majed telling my uncle in the living room that he could tolerate me no longer, that the problem was no more just a family matter, but had become something of concern for the whole neighborhood. Everyone seemed to know—everyone in the Lebanese community. He then told him about the time I ran away after he had found fault with some small thing in my behavior.

I remembered how it had been as I ran quickly and how my perspiration and the heat had enveloped me. As I went down the still unsurfaced road, I could see Majed coming after me. I began to go faster, hurling insults over my shoulder and using language that would normally have made me cringe. I shouted my insults as loudly as I could, especially when I noticed how someone had opened a window to try to see what was causing the uproar. All the people who lived on that street were Lebanese. Their houses had the appearance of shacks: wooden, jammed together, reeking with food smells. I thought of the smell of my mother's kitchen: fried onions, coriander with garlic. From time to time I heard the sound of meat being ground, reminding me of the last time I ate *kibbé* on an earlier occasion when I ran away from Majed's house. That had been on the day when Majed asked me to turn down the volume of our radio in front of our neighbor, who was calling on us for the first time. I was sitting on the balcony that led off the small kitchen, and when I refused, Majed came out to turn down the knob himself. I went raving mad. I raised the sound to its maximum, and various heads at once popped out of the windows in the neighboring houses. Majed gripped my arm and tried to force me back into the kitchen. I refused to move, and as the situation grew more unpleasant, so the neighbor grew more embarrassed. When Majed tried to speak to me, I screamed and ran out of the house.

There was an elderly woman, holding her long dress by its hem as she wrung the water out of it and surveyed her washing. She asked whether I was from the south. I sat on a slab of rock beside her washing and bent my head on my knees and cried. She turned to me to ask why I was crying. Did I miss my parents? I nodded. Gently, she said to me, "Come, my daughter, come into my house. I'll serve you some rose water."

I followed her and, entering her home, saw three children

sitting on the floor and eating. As she headed towards the kitchen she remarked, "These are my daughter's children. I look after them while my daughter is working with her husband in their store."

Then she gave me some *kibbé,* which I took willingly. As I began to eat it, I heard a knocking on the door.

Book Two

The Torrents of War

The voice of the newscaster Sharif Al-Akhawi, grown so familiar since the battles first raged in our streets, repeated over and over in its plebeian accent, "We are with you." As he said it again and again, my hand automatically went to my face and I started to pick at my pimples, all the while knowing how my day would end, my tomorrow begin: sitting and giving my mother a hand in the kitchen. Eating her food, what's more. I have put on so much weight that I look like a different person. The only resemblance between Zahra now and Zahra as she was are the scabs on her face.

People tell me I have put on weight because I left Africa. Those who are a little more forthright say that I have regained my health since leaving my husband, who, in their opinion, ill-treated me.

Poor Majed! How I've allowed them to draw conclusions about you! What if I were to tell them the truth—that it's only the food which makes me fat, that it's only because of the food that I can go on living, enduring the noises of the bombs and the bullets which penetrate everything—wood, rock, air, flesh? I watch my mother, waddling about and making sure that the wooden shutters are secured, the words which her lips speak never varying: "God save us!"

My father lights one cigarette after another, puffing at them in irritation and surrounding himself with a suffocating cloud of smoke. He goes to the radio, changes stations in the hope of hearing someone announce a cease-fire: hour after hour he sits in his striped pajamas. Nothing cuts across our daily canvas, nothing except for the food we eat and the noise of rockets shrieking before they burst. It never occurs to me that one of them might explode in our home—terrible things happen only to others.

Here I am, sitting on the edge of the bed in the room my brother Ahmad used to share with me, trying hard to read a story, *The Willow Tree,* as my father presses his transistor radio against his ear and walks slowly about, his head tilted to one side. He looks as if he has just had his appendix removed. He changes stations continuously, nervously. And I sit and read, hearing Sharif tell us not to leave our homes —"the Chiah road and Bourj al-Brajneh are unsafe."

My mother comes into the room and says, "We still have a whole sack of flour. We can survive a month without needing anything else."

A month, two months, what's the difference? I also think: one year, two years, what difference does it make? And what is there outside this house except for anxiety, worry and sorrow? Here I am totally relaxed. I see no one. I speak as little as possible to my mother, and then only about food. The moment night falls I sleep soundly. That is why it surprises me to hear my mother say, in the morning, that she hasn't been able to sleep a wink for the noise of fighting going on all night.

We had grown used to the idea of a cease-fire at the beginning. We did not dare to think or believe that fighting meant war any more than a cease-fire meant peace. We did not know what to think or say, even about the front being an inferno. Those were merely words, "the front," "peace" and "battle," all meaning the same thing: war. But we didn't think of ourselves as being in a war: we evaded the truth. Wishful thinking blossomed, our hopes ran high. When an announcement of a cease-fire was made, the women would set up their howlings of joy as rifle shots filled the air in celebration and young and old hurried barefoot into the street. Some returned home bearing packages and boxes of shopping, others carried loaves of bread. Even I ventured out with my neighbor Mariam, content just to buy ointment for my acne and thinking how the unnatural calm must show that something was wrong.

My forebodings would turn out to be justified when, before long, the cease-fire broke down and Sharif's voice told us despairingly, "The 'gentlemen' have begun to fight again. All roads are blocked and dangerous. Battles rage fiercely. The front lines are infernoes!"

At that point I felt a sense of relief. I stopped wondering what would become of me. I knew that I was at home, just as everyone else was at home and taking refuge, no matter who they were. Even the beautiful women we saw in the society pages of the magazines were in the same fix, hiding in some corner of their elegant homes, hearing what I heard, thinking what I thought.

When I heard that the battles raged fiercely and every front was an inferno, I felt calm. It meant that my perimeters were fixed by these walls, that nothing which my mother hoped for me could find a place inside them. The idea of my marrying again was buried deep by the thunder and lightning of the rockets. But it was all sick thinking, I would tell myself. My deep sleeping was a sickness, my devouring huge quantities of food was a sickness, my increasing weight, my wearing only my housecoat for two months on end were sicknesses. The scabs on my face that spread to my neck, to my shoulders, and my not caring about them, were a sickness. My silence was a sickness. My mother would launch into a tirade whenever she saw me in my housecoat during those two months, but I stayed completely silent. My indifference to her anxieties, especially when she tried to get out of me my real reason for divorcing Majed, was also a sickness.

I used to answer that the subject was over and done with, so far as I was concerned. But she remained unconvinced and expressed her annoyance in reproaches and bitterness, mocking my pimples and my madness. Still I stayed silent whenever the subject of Majed came up. In my mind I had named him "Africa," and used to wonder what had taken me to that remote country in the first place.

Africa had been the shaft of a deep well down which I had hidden my threadbare secret. I had come back no more than half a human being. My nervous fits, which had increased while I was there, did not completely disappear after my return. They had taken their toll of me, making me realize that I was not an easy person to cope with. I began to act as though I were molded out of a rigid material, incapable of either expansion or contraction.

From that point on I never allowed anyone to peep in through the narrow opening by which I viewed the world outside. I blocked off every aperture through which anyone might try to reach or touch me.

Once Malek saw me alone on a bus. He turned his face away. My own reaction to seeing him was to press my thighs together tightly and grip hard on the package of wool which I carried. I felt as unyielding as wood, and stayed like that for many days, until a cease-fire was announced.

Then I panicked. I knew I would go to pieces the moment the rockets' noise dwindled. The cease-fire meant I could no longer stay in bed for hours on end, or wander aimlessly about the kitchen as the radio blared. The cease-fire meant having to leave the house. It meant going outside, and seeing people, and they seeing me for what I was. My mother's voice would grow shrill: "Come on, girl! Take off your housecoat. Get out and see the world. Go and see the face of God's world."

Silently I used to ask: "Why should I do so? No one matters to me any more. I am better than any of them. What will I see there except lies and hypocrisy?"

I thought it seriously, even bitterly. I included all my relatives in a category with the rest of the world. I couldn't talk to them, not even to say, "How are you?" They showed their sarcasm, because of my fat, because of my acne. They never tried to get to know me and see me for the person I really was. They cared only about appearance, and mine had gone to the dogs.

With tears in her eyes, my mother would beg me, "Have pity on yourself, on your youthfulness. Have a word with your aunt. Respond to your cousin. May God preserve you. Slip in and say hello to our neighbor Zainab."

I would stay quietly in bed, refusing to leave my room. My mother would open the door stealthily and repeat her pleas over and over, each time in a different wheedling tone until I became so irritated that I swore at her and at those who tried to visit me. I would shout to her face, "So-and-so has come only to see my madness. They're here to laugh at the state I'm in, not because they love me." And my voice would rise to such a pitch that whoever sat waiting in the living room would become embarrassed and leave. After a while, no one had the courage to call to try speaking to me. If it so happened that I was in the living room when a visitor arrived, and they heard me answer some incidental question, they would look up incredulously, scarcely believing that I sounded normal and could speak normal words.

Our home seemed different during the day from how it was at night. In the morning, it would be filled with bustling daily routines. The beds, the dining-room chairs, the pictures on the walls, the pots and pans in the kitchen, the pots of basil and red peppers lined up on the window sill, the smell of the food that drifted from the kitchen to my bedroom: all these were as they had been before the war. But at night the place changed. It became a haunted citadel. The thunder of artillery reverberated off the walls, the shriek of rockets pierced our ears and reached our very core, and our peaceful refuge came to be filled with phantoms of fear and the sound of bullets.

As day followed day and night followed night, the overheard voices grew louder, their tempo quickened. A bed was no longer a place in which to find peace and rest. Fear loomed and intensified as the voices outside grew louder. Eventually I came to hate my bed, and could no longer sleep in it as deeply as I had at the beginning when the fury of the shooting had only made me feel quiet and sleepy. Now, in spite of my belief that everything that happened in the night would evaporate with sunrise, I woke up riddled with aches, as if, during the night on my bed, two men had beaten me with whips. I would get up, feeling as if my bones were shattered, unable to move. Blue veins developed under my eyes, making them seem as if bruised.

I would walk about the house, which had been a night-mare in the darkness, and feel totally surprised that all remained so normal. Fear and portents mingled with the hope that everything might soon end. Those days drew me closer to my mother and father, who seemed to realize, for the first time, that I was not a specter. I began to follow the news of the war, reading nervously but eagerly between the lines in the newspapers, searching for the truth. Then I would overflow with despair and disbelief. All those figures which listed the numbers killed, could they be possible? Were there truly these kidnappings? Did they actually check your identity card and then, on the basis of your religion, either kill you or set you free? Were the young people who fought in the war receiving orders from their leaders, and were they wearing combat clothes? Was it true that the Rivoli Cinema had been burnt down? Was it true about the fire in the Souk Sursok? And the one in Souk Al-Tawile? How could you tell if someone was really a sniper? Had George, the hair-dresser, our neighbor, turned against me? Had I turned against him? I could not believe my ears when I heard my mother say: "God curse these Christians!"

My father turned on her and reproached her, "You are so ignorant, woman! You will always be ignorant! This is a war between nations, not between Christian and Moslem, woman!"

Is all this truly happening outside our walls? And does life still continue as it used to before the war? Is all this truly happening in Lebanon? No sooner does the shooting stop than people make a dash for the cafés on Hamra Street. The corner of Al-Mazraa becomes crowded with sesame seed buns vendors, the road to Sidon lined with people selling lettuces and radishes. The press photographers take pictures

of life during the cease-fire, and a leading newspaper cap-
tions one of those pictures, "If traffic jams mean something!"

How can people forget the nightmare overnight? How
can they run smiling out of their homes, as though the
deaths that happened only the day before occurred in some
other country? Suddenly I shudder as it seems clear to me
that everything in our lives is on the verge of disintegration.
I ought to refuse to scrub the floor or prepare the food,
make the bed or water the plant pots. I should let everything in the place die a slow death, and my father and
mother would also do better if they stopped eating and living, for why should life continue inside the home when
everything outside is collapsing? The apartment itself should
fall down, too. Then it could be seen how war pervades the
whole of Lebanon.

Yet everything *is* true! I seize the hand of my brother
Ahmad, who, having disappeared for a whole year, has returned wearing combat uniform and carrying a rifle. He has
grown a beard and informs us he is stationed in Al-Chiah. I
pounce on him and shake him, shouting incredulously that
this is Ahmad. Yet can it be the same boy who used to steal
my chocolate, who used to bite and then kiss me? Who
used to frighten me when I went to the bathroom and tell
me how, behind every picture, there lurked a demon waiting to pounce? Is this the Ahmad who would hide under
the bed with me, especially after ink had been accidentally
spilled on the carpet, who would peel an orange, leaving
the skin intact, and then stuff it with Kleenex? The Ahmad
who told me jokes about elephants and ants, who once gave
me ten liras to go to the dermatologist to try to get my acne
cleared up?

Now he stands before us, sporting his combat suit and his

beard. Why? How has it come about? I cannot believe it. I scream and grab at him as he tries to judge whether his sister is really as mad as he has been told.

Only then do I realize that I am fainting, that my eyes are closing. Later I find myself lying on my bed, my mother beside me as she cries silently and holds my hand. My father is sitting there too, gazing at me. I realize I need to go to the bathroom. My mother helps. I get up, and as I pass the kitchen table I see that it has 200 liras lying on its surface and wonder who they belong to. But, too weak to give the matter further thought, I return to bed.

My mother comes and sits beside me once more. She holds my hand and says, "I hope, God willing, you feel better now."

I nod, as my father remains seated and vacant, his head bowed. I ask my mother whether she knows what Ahmad is up to. When she nods her head, indicating both yes and no, I ask her, "Why, Mamma? Why?" And she moans, with tears in her eyes, "Oh, my daughter, oh!"

I think how I must develop some control over my nerves so that I can ask Ahmad why he has become involved with this war which I do not understand. I ask my mother whether Ahmad will go on visiting us, in spite of the way I have behaved. She half-smiles and says comfortingly, "Don't worry now, Zahra. Are you not brother and sister? He realizes you're a nervous type."

Then I ask when he will come again, and she replies, "He'll be back after the cease-fire. Then he'll come home and rest. Oh, my poor boy!"

At this point my father jerks up his head and says sarcastically, "Oh, poor boy indeed! Running around with a rifle, the idiot! Who does he think he is fighting? His brother, his friend, his neighbor! We are all Lebanese, you foolish woman. We are all one family! Lebanon is a small country. The pity of it! Their minds are deranged. If it were not so great a disgrace, I would have slung him into the street. For God's sake, what does he imagine? That you were happy to receive two hundred liras? I wouldn't touch such cursed money. It belongs to martyrs and orphans. You did wrong in accepting it."

The war goes on. Its upheavals shake up the living and the dead. Sharif's voice is heard no longer. All the voices of the airwaves have commingled and dispersed simultaneously. Numerous broadcasting systems, various television channels, all assume a sole legitimacy.

Our street, once ruled by the spirit of life, now has death for its overlord. Somewhere in the lower half of the street there lives a sniper who perches on top of one of the vacated blocks.

How is it that death has come to rule over half the street, directing that a child will fall, a man or a woman will fall, each with a bullet in the brain, each one alive and moving, even laughing or crying, at the very moment when they walked into the sniper's sights? How is it that Abu Jamil's restaurant still stands across the street from us and gives off its smell of hummus while those who go in at its doors carry ammunition?

Outside our window the war had shown me dozens of young men, blindfolded, walking before the muzzles of the Kalashnikov rifles whose butts had beaten them earlier; Kalashnikovs carried by young warriors who had, before the war, been in schools and at work, who had loitered at the only café and restaurant in our quarter. On that particular day they were herding their prisoners into the basement of the apartment block which faced ours. Trembling, I told my mother that the things we had been reading about were now actually happening on our street. I cried out, "What shall we do?" and began to look for my shoes. I'd even forgotten their color and shape, not having worn them for an entire month.

But my mother stood, barring my way and asking, "Are we all off our heads?"

I pushed her aside and, going to the window, stared across at the entrance where two guards stood sipping coffee. I recognized them as two young men who had been pupils in my class at high school. I felt relieved. Surely they would listen to me and save those inside. I ran to the door, but my mother blocked my path, threatening and screaming and shouting to my father in the bathroom. I turned back and flung open the window, calling out the young men's names. They turned to look, but even though I cried out my name to them, they didn't remember who I was. One of them came across to the window. The expression on his face relaxed. He said, *"Ahlein*—greetings." I asked who the young men were whom they had taken inside. He answered: "You know who."

"What have they done?"

"Nothing. We stopped them at the barricades. We would like to exchange them for others."

"God's blessing be yours. Let them return to their homes."

"What?"

"God's blessing on you. Let them return to their homes. Let them go free. Can't you show pity? What have they done? May God's blessing be yours. Let them return home."

I felt myself being torn from the window as my mother's hand covered my mouth and my father's grip dragged me backwards. I heard them both shout, perhaps in unison for the first time ever, "Dear God, have you gone crazy? Have you gone mad? Would you like them to kill you? Perhaps, if they do, we'll be safe and free from your shame. You are crazy. They will make you pay dearly for this."

I sat there, weeping and helpless. I held my head in both hands and cried. I prayed not to hear the sound of firing. I begged God not to let me hear any noise of killing from outside. As time went on and I still heard nothing, I thought of the captive young men, sitting in darkness. I thought of their fear at hearing shots. I wondered what went on in their minds. If only my mother would let me go to them. I sat behind the window, expecting to glimpse them, but saw only the changing of the guards. There was no sound from inside the building.

I sat on, punishing myself, feeling guilty for all the times when I had felt uncomfortable before the war, and for all the misery which I had thought was misery before the war, and the pain which I had thought was pain before the war.

Perhaps, at the time, all such feelings had been real enough. But if I were to measure my pain in Africa and place it beside the agony the war created, then no comparison was possible. The sufferings of war continued their endless flow, palpable suffering with concrete evidence: the corpses and mutilation, the fire and devastation.

I could do nothing except volunteer myself at the hospital. Our neighbor's daughter and I had to walk close to the walls for fear of the sniper, hidden away on the rooftop of the near-by building. I was constantly afraid that he would get me, even though his field of fire lay in the other direction.

I lasted only three days at the hospital. I was no use to anyone, with my constant trembling and my soul permeated with the groans of the wounded. The smell of the blood mixed with the stench of excrement, the buzzing of hundreds of flies as big as birds, the laments of the relatives and parents of the wounded, all entered me as if saturating the very plasma that ran in my veins. Those who speak of war in platitudes have never seen a war. Those who have only seen wars and hospitals in movies have seen nothing of the truth.

I wondered whether the leaders of the factions ever visited hospitals, and if they did, even for an hour, how they could then live an ordinary day again? Could they stop themselves thinking of an amputated leg? Or of an eye that had turned to liquid? Or of a severed hand lying there in resignation and helplessness? Why did none of those leaders, as they stood listening to the groans, pledge to put a stop to the war and cry out, "This war shall end! I shall finish it! No cause can be won until the war is stopped. No cause comes before the cause of humanity and safety. The war ends here and now!"

Silence reigned in our house. Silence reigned everywhere. I waited for the men to reappear outside the dark basement door. I did not heed my father's shouts as he warned me to keep clear of the window, to close the shutter before they shot me. I could not hear the sound of any firing. The captives were still alive, waiting to be exchanged for other kidnapped hostages. Then I heard a shot. Another shot. A third shot. But they did not seem to be coming from close by. Could they have come from the basement, or did I imagine it? The basement door looked the same. The two armed guards paid no attention to the sound of gunfire. Those bullets did not even have any effect on Ahmad when he dropped by one afternoon after it had come to seem to me that you could expect nothing but death.

The night before I had forced my heart, hiding behind my ribs, down below my belly. I could feel a vast emptiness where my heart had been. The vacuum dragged on my lungs to the point where I could no longer breathe, the air leaking in all directions. And I felt as if my heart had left me, for how long I don't know, as I lay, submitting to death, with painful resignation. The rockets poured like fireworks and the din moved directly overhead. For a moment my mother and I thought the ceiling was about to fall in and that we would be thrown to the ground to become just like a photograph in the papers: a whole family killed playing cards, still clutching the cards in their hands, the shrapnel mingling with parts of their bodies, everything else looking normal, children's underwear still hanging in the room.

My mother and I shouted out together as if we were once again as close as orange and navel, as we had been when we stood trembling behind the door, back in my earliest memories. Now she moved across from one corner to the other as the room was lit up by explosions. We crawled down to the basement, the noise all the while moving closer until it was as though it had its source inside my head. Before I could cry out, an explosion had burst near-by and my heart had dropped between my feet. I was left completely empty, except for my voice, but even this I could not control any more. I lifted my head and saw my mother crying like a child, hiding her face in her hands, unable to move an inch. As I lifted up my head, the lights came back on, showing us where we were, showing us we were still alive. I wondered, "Is our home under observation? Are they trying to kill us?" But those rockets had come from various directions. It was not that our house alone was a target. The whole region, all the buildings in Beirut, all the people of the city, were a target. The roar of battle resumed.

Now I could understand nothing. I screamed. I stood up nervously, ready to meet death. My mother pulled at my legs. I stood there, screaming, screaming, screaming. And when her hands started to tear at my legs, I kicked her. But she didn't care. She continued to follow me, crawling on the floor and tearing at my legs, hoping to get me to listen to her and lie down. She wanted me to accept that treacherous space between those treacherous walls and under those treacherous lights as my hiding place.

When the noise roared again, I could no longer control myself and ran for the basement door, hoping to escape. I trembled from head to foot as my heart pounded, and only when I reached the hallway between the elevator and our apartment did I breathe again. The lights were dim, but so was the noise. The explosions seemed to be muffled, at a distance. I sat on the bottom step of the stairs which I loved so much, the stairs whose shapes I had forgotten.

By the time my mother reached me and saw me, her eyes were almost starting out of her head. I suppose she had never expected to find me alive. For one second she must have thought I had gone mad and was roaming the streets. As she sat down next to me I found myself burying my face in her shoulder as I cried for fear and love. She hugged me, enveloping me in her arms, and said, "Tomorrow we go to the village. Don't cry, my darling."

Then heavy footsteps came closer and I heard my father saying, "By God, you're probably in the best place," as he came to see how we were getting on, having emerged from his own hiding place with the concierge on the ground floor. My mother asked him whether we could go to the village. He looked away for a moment, then looked back at us. I could see, in the glimmer, how much he had changed. He was no longer a fat monster on whose chest and shoulders black hairs curled like cockroaches. I noticed how thin his body had become, and how his head had developed a constant trembling, just like an old man who used to sit outside our school, selling yellow pulses. Had anyone else noticed this constant tremor? Had my mother realized how quickly he was ageing?

He looked at us as his head trembled slightly and asked, "What about Ahmad? How can we leave that worthless fool behind? How can we persuade Ahmad to throw down his arms and come with us?"

But when Ahmad arrived, I did not dare to open my mouth. He also had grown terribly thin, and, as soon as he saw us, he broke down in tears and hugged each of us in turn. He couldn't believe he was home. My father avoided him and kept at a distance as if my brother carried some contagion. Ahmad collapsed into the first chair he saw and could not lift his eyes from his own muddy boots as he spoke: "I've been under the influence of the combat groups. It's a different story being on your own than it is being part of a large group. To belong in a group makes you part of the war and not a murderer. Your gun isn't a gun, but an object you carry naturally. And the group digests you so that you forget you are an individual. I was standing in the open, at the door of a bire, and the bullets seemed unreal, like bullets from toys. It is the combat groups who are responsible for everything that's happened, not you or I." I began to weep hysterically and to ask Ahmad why he was telling us all this. I held out my arms to him and was shocked to see Ahmad still Ahmad, despite his battle uniform, his beard, the glazed look in his eyes. Here was the same Ahmad who had left his home to go and fight. No sooner did he return to it than he became a part of it again, a member of the family.

My mother disappeared into the kitchen, soon returning with some food on a tray. Even now Ahmad was given the lion's share of meat, despite us being at war. Ahmad may have been in battle, but to my mother he was still a child. My father turned to face us, and I had never seen him so feeble. He could hardly speak for weakness as his head went on shaking and he tried to persuade Ahmad to leave everything and go with us to the village. To my amazement, Ahmad agreed. I put aside my fear and shyness and, seeing only the old Ahmad, ran to clasp him with joy.

But he never did leave. He never came with us to the village. The war was like a weevil that had found its way into the heart of a huge bag of white flour and settled there. And I, likewise, was destined not to stay in the village. I would return to Beirut at the first opportunity, to be overtaken by that same weevil, back in the midst of the fighting.

But those who lived in the villages were surprised to have news of what was taking place in Beirut and Tripoli. When they spoke about the war, it was as though they mentioned cities of no direct interest to themselves. It had no place in their lives. Their days were passed as usual. They took care of their routine needs and ignored the war which raged only a few kilometers away.

In Beirut and Tripoli there was no such monotony. Daily needs there were reduced to the barest minimum. No one thought about what food to eat or when to clean the house or take a bath. No one cared whether or not a certain detergent washed linen cleaner or whiter. Such concerns had been blown apart by the flames of guns and bombs. But people in the villages continued to pursue their daily strug--

gles from crack of dawn to the end of the day, when they and the sun slept.

I felt no reaction at all at seeing the village houses again or the childhood friends who had grown up and who must have heard many tales about me. But when I saw how the tobacco booth was still as it had been when I was a child, and saw the girls being covered by the tobacco leaves as they worked and laughed mischievously, and felt the same warm wind, then I realized how I had never really left either the village or that booth. Only when that inner sadness took hold of me did I realize that my grandfather was no longer present. His chair remained, however, even if its bamboo strips were unraveling.

And the very pond from which my *Qarina* once called my name and frightened me was still there. I didn't walk down to it, but went instead to a place where the piece of waste land began and found it just as I had last seen it, with dried weeds and dried bushes. From a distance the sun shone on it, showing a few scattered graves near the roadside. In among those graves lay that of my grandfather. The last time I had seen him was when they laid his body on top of a wooden table in the Ali Mahdi's garden. They left him there, with only a towel to cover his legs and a few trees to cast their shadows over him. There he waited for a man to come and wash him one last time, and I have never cried as I did then: when I saw him lying on the table as the men stood about, chatting and sipping coffee as though they were having a good time, as though they would not soon be walking solemnly behind his coffin.

I knew I was going to have to leave the village and return to Beirut. It didn't feel right to be taking refuge here, far from Ahmad. It didn't feel right that the war should be

taking place in another part of the country while my grandfather's friends and the villagers on the frontier took such
pains with the way they looked, sitting among the tobacco
booths amid the scent of the south. Dozens waited to cross
the frontier to sell their harvests in Israel, as if life was, in all
respects, normal and natural and there was no one to question what they did, not even the young men fighting in
Beirut.

If only my Aunt Khadija could have seen it. If only she
could have known how the frontier was now open between
the village and Zion, as we called the occupied territories.
Her daughter, Fadila, had married in Palestine before the
war of 1948. And so, when Palestine was lost, Fadila was
lost also. My Aunt Khadija waited for her each day, and
with each day which passed another bit of her mind seemed
to go. Despite the unruffled life of the village, rumors developed concerning Fadila and her whereabouts. At times
people said she had been seen in the village of Kaffar Tibnit,
at others in Aita Al-Foukhar, and my Aunt Khadija would
hurry barefoot over pebbles and through thornbushes to try
to catch up with these mirages of her daughter.

As soon as she realized that a rumor was only a mirage,
she would beat her head against a rock and slap her face in
self-punishment. Her mind was on the verge of cracking,
her sense of reality confused. My aunt embraced the
thought of the illusory Fadila and sang to herself long
monologues filled with yearning for her daughter. She even
lost her true name in this pursuit of her daughter and the
knocking of her head against the rocks when the villagers
jokingly nicknamed her "The Waiting One." She began to
conceal all her belongings in a jute sack, suspended about
her waist. She would roam through the villages of the

neighborhood, begging a few piastres here and there and filling her sack with them. Then they nicknamed her "The Stuffed One."

If only my aunt could have known how men journeyed to the other side, into the occupied territories, how women gave birth there . . . But my aunt lay before me in her grave, under its modest white stone.

I wanted to return to Beirut, but not because I could accept that any one faction fighting in the civil war was more right than another. Ahmad and his friends claimed to be fighting against exploitation. Anxious to draw attention to the demands of the repressed Shi'ite minority, they wanted to destroy imperialism along with the isolationist forces and the decaying, tattered régime. But their beautiful words never killed imperialism, while they remained behind their barricades, facing buildings and shops and the barricades of their opponents. Bullets flew, bombs exploded, smoke rose and bodies bled, but none of it did a thing to touch the decaying régime.

I had never believed that the quiet streets I knew so well could ever change into a battlefield. But now those formerly neutral streets were suddenly filled with a spirit of revenge and tension. I could never understand how the fighters themselves, whatever side they were on, could take aim and fire in those streets. Were they all drugged, like Ahmad and his friends? Did they come with glazed eyes and forget how they had once walked the streets in safety? And now, in broad daylight as well as in night's darkness they murdered in those same streets.

Ahmad's friends would be semi-drugged and languid when they visited, and I never dared to ask them my questions. They belonged to a world that was not my world, not a world for those who dared not lift a gun. Always, to my great surprise, they would be laughing like young men in a dormitory. I could never understand their logic. It was a logic which confused war with life.

I could never ask them whether it was that war had become a habit for them, a part of their daily routine; or how they could move about in the empty city at night and see all that destruction. Didn't they realize how, in the yard of the building opposite, trucks stopped to unload stolen goods? Silence was one response. Another was, "No one can have complete control over those who take part in a revolution." I watched them as they sprawled out and relaxed and laughed and exchanged jokes. Then they would go away, leaving me certain that I could never grasp the pattern of their thoughts or their reasons for participating.

When news stopped coming from my parents in the mountains, I felt convinced that news from Ahmad and me had also stopped reaching them. I made the war my excuse for not joining them, as I had promised. I began to notice changes in my personality and in the way Ahmad's friends treated me. They all looked on me as a sister, discussing and talking openly in front of me, in spite of the fact that my tenseness had led me to let fly at them at times.

Once I was woken by a noise. Strange cries mingled with children's voices. I ran to the window to see scores of women with children and sacks and various belongings on their backs. Their screams were high-pitched, their dresses hitched up to their waists, their swollen bellies supporting dangling breasts. Everything about the scene seemed strange, perhaps because I had tried to get up earlier but couldn't, for my *Qarina* had been tormenting me while I was asleep.

There had been earlier sounds, but I hadn't even been able to open my eyes. My *Qarina* crouched in one of the room's corners and watched me. She had arrived in the company of a man whose features I couldn't make out clearly. The weight of his body had contradicted any thought that I might be dreaming. The weight of his body on mine had given me a faint shiver. It was as though he held a peacock's feather and tickled me with its iridescent green and blue eye. The feather moved all over my body until it reached my lower regions. I felt myself shiver with pleasure under the gaze of my *Qarina* as she watched me from her corner. Whenever I longed to complete a shiver, to reach my climax, I felt embarrassed by her presence. The weight of the man's body was on my breasts while, in the lower part of my abdomen, I felt the peacock's feather. And, outside, the sounds increased to a higher pitch. I thought the voices must be an invention by my *Qarina* to get me out of bed. The noises didn't cease, however, but grew louder and more varied. The crying of children began to be mixed in with them.

My eyes would not open, they were so heavy, and their lids were glued shut. I tried to rise, but the man's weight pressed down on my breasts and on all my body except for my lower abdomen where the feather kept on tickling. I began to raise my hips, following the feather's movements, pleading for it not to go away from the lower part of my abdomen. And as soon as I had felt the need to move, I needed to move more and more, to submit to my ecstasy, even though I was still aware of my *Qarina* lurking in the shadows, and of the noises in the street, the bleeping of car horns. Suddenly I was looking at the wall on the other side of the room and sensing how quiet the house had grown. The sun was streaming in at the windows and all at once there was no trace of either my *Qarina* or the man. The peacock feather became one among many in the fan which hung on the wall.

It was then that I made out the voices and ran to the window to see the crowd of women and children. They were talking to the militia from our quarter, and everyone seemed to be caught up in a raging argument directly outside the basement doorway of the apartment block opposite: that entrance for death and larceny. Having got dressed, I locked our apartment door and went down the stairs, still sensing the man's weight on my body.

The sunlight dazzled my eyes, as if I was seeing it for the first time in years. I felt an urge to run out, as I was, into the crowd, carefree, unconstrained by the mass of people. I tried to blank out the screams, the shrieks and wails. The women were screaming because they had just come from the Karantina camp after a battle between their men and the Phalangists. Still not knowing the fate of their men, the women and children had been herded into a fleet of buses to move them from the eastern to the western part of the city. Our street had received its quota of refugees from a bus which had disgorged its contents early in the morning. The militia responsible for the quarter was attempting to reach some agreement, but to no avail. The children were bawling, knowing nothing of what was going on. The young man in charge was attempting to exercise some control, especially after all the residents came out and surrounded the refugees from east Beirut.

But chaos increased with every moment, and the militia chief, growing ever more desperate, stood on the top of one of the vehicles, drew his revolver and fired it into the air. The voices fell silent at once. "Now," the chief of militia said very quickly, "we understand that the buses will take

you to the beach, to the beach cabins there. Each mother is
to collect her children and belongings and wait in silence. Is
that clear? No noise! Whoever utters a word will be left
behind."

He jumped off the vehicle. It never occurred to me to
think how these people were homeless, cut off from their
past and carrying bitter memories so vivid they could never
be forgotten. It never occurred to me that, with my parents
away and me living by myself, I could have taken in at least
one family. It never occurred to me to offer my services, no
matter how limited they might have been.

Only after a few days had gone by did I begin to think
about what I might have done. What was needed to make
one person's pain stronger than another's? Why had I stood
like a tourist, watching what went on before my eyes as if it
was all happening to remote strangers? Was this the same
process which overtook Ahmad and his comrades after they
had run out of bullets and grenades? When the time came
for them to relax and to stand down from their positions for
several hours, did they see themselves as having had nothing
to do with the war, while people still crouched in their
homes and shelters?

Such contradictions became a torture to me, as did those
concerning my relationship with the sniper high up on the
building down the street. However am I to describe that
relationship? It began with me climbing the stairs to find
him and feeling life start to revive in me. I had taken a
yellow plastic bag and told my prying neighbor I was going
out to buy some vegetables. As I walked down the street, I
was like one without a heart, for my heart had dropped
again between my feet. I anticipated only one thing: hearing
a bullet and then falling dead to the ground like the others
the sniper had killed on the other side of the street. I

stopped at one of the barricades and moved my head as if hypnotized. Nothing that was happening seemed real and the drops of sweat dripped from all of me, even my eyebrows on to my feet, between which lay my heart.

When I came to the crossroads, I saw the apartment building, seeming so safe and quiet, its windows shut, its curtains and venetian blinds drawn. A small date tree stood at its entrance. By that point my heart had been left behind altogether. I could no longer feel my pulse and my body moved without thought or sensation. In that critical moment I said to myself, "Well, here I am. I am about to lose myself for ever. Will I hear the shot first, or will I fall before I hear the shot?"

But there I was, still on my feet. Nothing had happened, and when I looked up towards the sky-line of the building, I saw nothing. I looked behind me and noticed a sheet of corrugated iron stuck in the ground. On it was written, "Beware! Sniper." I looked up again and saw the air above as empty as the street below.

As I mounted the stairs, life slowly flowed back into me. The semi-darkness damped down the dust of the years. My feet, while dragging, seemed to grow strangely light. The higher I went, the more I held up my head. Yet still I saw nothing. If he had spotted me through his sights, then why did he stay in hiding? Or was he concentrating on watching the enemy lines? Perhaps he had recognized my navy dress from when I had last put it on a week ago. Or my plastic yellow bag. Had he recognized me from my distraught and frightened face? Or was he relieving himself in one of the roof corners? Was it a normal thing that I was doing, closing all doors of escape behind me?

I had made myself into an easy target for assassination, so what had become of all the fear which used to envelop me as a child? I used to cower, holding my breath till I practically suffocated. Where was the fear I once had of entering the kitchen at night; the fear of the two genies who lurked outside the window, hanging there in the air? And my fear at my mother's screams, which still rang in my ears and echoed in my heart? In spite of being so young, I had smelled her fear and absorbed it as if I were a sponge washed up and dried out on the beach.

Then, all at once, the very same fear pinned me to the ground as I heard the sound of footsteps and my heart once again plummeted. The footsteps reverberated in the sea of silence, in the corners where death crouched in the building of the lone sniper. The fear spilled into the street, drifted into the empty apartments behind their closed wooden shutters and ran along the balconies. The footsteps belonged to a soul which knew only the pulse-beat of death; that knew only the void. I was alone with a fear I couldn't quite manage to grasp. Was it the kind of fear that came to the sane or to the mad? I waited to be obliterated by the sound of those footsteps. I stood there, anticipating earthquake and explosion. But I had never expected such soft footfalls. Looking up, I could make out a face in the darkness. It was a face which I recognized, already familiar to me. Then I heard his voice: "Did anyone see you come up here?"

I made no reply. I had been standing there petrified, but now all fear disappeared with the sound of his voice. Here was, after all, another human being, who had thoughts and asked questions. Who was Lebanese. Who knew where the Pigeon Rock—our lovers' leap—stood. Who knew where the taxi stand was located.

He came down a few more steps, and now I could see him clearly. I continued to clutch at the yellow plastic bag, held tight against my thigh. His voice moved closer, and with it his body. I could smell the heavy scent of his perspiration. He put a hand on my breast and then removed it as I went on peering hard at his features in the half-light. He must have begun to undo his trousers with one hand as he started to knead my shoulder with the other.

Then, in one move, he pounced on me and pushed me on to the stairs. He lifted my dress to the waist. He spread out his body on mine without even taking off my knickers. He did not seem to mind that he made my back and side hurt, and though I twisted about with discomfort, he paid no attention. He came quite quickly, shuddering briefly in his spasm of pleasure. Then he stood up, wiped himself off at his trouser opening and began to do up the buttons. At that point I got up too, aware of the hurt in my back and side and rubbing my limbs where the bones ached.

As I prepared to leave, I heard him say, "Tomorrow, at this time, I shall come to your apartment."

I shook my head vigorously, but as I went down the stairs he called after me, "It would be much better in your apartment."

"My brother Ahmad is always at my aunt's," I called back to him.

He took a deep breath, explaining, "I mean at *your* apartment, in the block which faces Abu Jamil's restaurant."

I went on down the stairs without answering. His footsteps faded above me. I gripped my plastic bag and held it close to my dress. I could feel a wetness on my thigh and at the edge of my knickers and wished the dripping might stop before it betrayed me.

At the foot of the staircase I paused a moment to gather some strength, then went out into the day's brightness. The street was as quiet as usual, so quiet you could have heard a pin fall. But no sooner had I gone past the corrugated-iron sheet which said "Beware! Sniper," and reached the cross-roads, than the street started to come alive with people. I began to walk more quickly, the empty yellow plastic bag against my thigh and dress to conceal the dampness from the sniper's seed, which still dripped down my upper thigh.

As I arrived at the entrance to our block, I breathed a sigh of relief, ran up the stairs and opened the door, as relaxed as if I had just heard the war had ended. The apartment was empty. A thread of happiness ran through me. I took off my clothes in the bathroom, then washed and dried myself, thinking of my father and mother and how their absence had made things easier.

Whenever, after that, I climbed the stairs of that quiet building, the doors of its abandoned apartments seemed to have ears behind them and my feet would scarcely touch the dusty stone treads. I never saw a soul at any time when I went up those stairs to reach the sniper, even though I had a sense of eyes accusing me in the darkness.

He grew accustomed to waiting for me at a set hour, and then could think only of my arrival. Hardly would I have lifted my eyes before I saw him smile. And before I could even reach the top step, he would pull me down beside him and eagerly cover my body with his own. As usual, however, I felt nothing more than his entering me, then thrusting inside me. Apart from that I felt no pleasure. I would look away, accepting his body yet not daring to speak a word as he lay on top of me; not wanting him to let go of me. Only in the second week of our meetings did I begin to feel a certain pleasure whenever he drew me down on to the ground. Feelings of security, of comfort, even of relaxation began to grow day by day, despite our conversation never going beyond his asking if I needed money or whether I took great care during my journey to meet him.

Once he took from his pocket 100 liras and tried to stick them in my bra strap. My chin trembled and I burst into tears. I groped for the money until I found it. He accepted it back, but said, "Please, I beg of you, don't cry. Someone might hear you. I realize you come from a good family and don't take money, but this is wartime."

I stood up to go home as I did each day, creeping away from our meetings like some kind of insect, aware of the wetness on my upper thigh. I would raise up my head as I went out into the light, but then crouch along in the street, trying to find as much shelter as possible, even though the sniper was the only god of death, the only threat in the locality. But who knew when some other god of death might not suddenly appear from nowhere? At the barricade my heart would stop beating as the young men who manned it yelled and screamed at me, "What are you doing, girl, coming from along there? Don't you know there's a sniper?" I never answered them, but kept silent all the way back home, where I would go in, lock the door securely and fling myself on the bed.

Days become long during wartime, but my days of war grew short. Each morning I would think about the afternoon and of meeting my sniper. Each night I would think of the warmth of his body on mine. A shudder of pleasure would run through me.

Whenever I stood up afterwards, and pulled down my skirt, he would hand me a paper tissue. I had never dared to wipe my thighs in his presence, even though he would courteously turn his back on me. I would keep those tissues in the palm of my hand. But once, when he turned to face me again, he fumbled in his shirt pocket and brought out a ring that shone in the half-light. He held it up and asked whether I thought it beautiful. When I said, "Yes," he

opened my palm and found the tissue there, so opened my
other palm and pressed the ring into it. I kept on squeezing
the ring with the one hand, the tissue with the other. Then,
to my surprise, I heard him speak my name. I had given
him my body, my chance of life or death, but never my
name. And I never did ask how he found it out.

At that point my father's image came into my mind,
shrunken, lacking the Hitler-like moustache and with no
watch in his trouser pocket. By now his heavy frame had
lost all sign of the brute strength with which he had beaten
my mother. His voice no longer carried a threat of thunder.
As the sniper drew me closer, I was totally submissive. He
spread me out in the narrow space in front of the doors that
led out on to the roof, lifted my skirt with one hand as the
fingers of his other secretly explored between my thighs.

I felt a sense of shame when he touched me, but, at the
same time, didn't want him to take his hand away. For the
first time I reached out my arms and pulled him even closer.
At that moment I wished that all the weight of the world
could be lying on top of me as his hand continued probing.
I shut my eyes and hugged him closer so that his weight
would become even greater. And whenever his hand
seemed about to depart, I would tense my thighs together
and urge it back into its trap. He understood my needs. His
hand began to move gently, and when I asked for more he
gave me more. And I wanted more, and he gave me more,
until I cried out.

My cries became like lava and hot sand pouring from a
volcano whose suffocating dust was burying my past life. It
blotted out the door to Dr. Shawky's clinic and the door
behind which we hid as my mother clutched at me in panic,
the fat face invading the dark, seeing yet not seeing us; and
being underneath the walnut tree, the man himself stretched

out with his head in her lap, while I felt cold in spite of the sun and the warmth of the brown stones. The darkness blotted out my mother and I didn't dare to call her. The man had locked the door, closed the green wooden shutters which overlooked the garden. He was not Dr. Shawky, was he? Perhaps he was. Did people change their shape from time to time? As my mother, in the darkness, removed her stockings and spoke to the man, the man reopened the shutters quietly. My mother hugged me and told me to stay under the shutters and not to go down and play in the garden. "Let no one see you. I'll not be long."

Before I could refuse and tell her how frightened I was, the man lifted me out on to the balcony which overlooked the garden. Before I could turn round and say anything else to my mother, the shutters were closed sharply. I was alone and trembling, afraid someone might ask me what I was doing there. I have no idea how long I stood there before I saw, at the end of the garden, a woman in a short dress hanging out washing, picking the clothespegs from her mouth and snapping them on to the line, then bending down and picking up more clothes and clothespegs. She couldn't see me as I shrank against the wall, but as she went to the other side of the line and turned around, she did notice me. Rather than come over, though, she disappeared. As soon as she did so, the shutters opened and the man lifted me back into the room. I saw the woman again in the distance, speaking to another who had her hair covered with a white kerchief . . .

My cries as I lay in the dust, responding to the sniper's exploring fingers, contained all the pain and sickness from my past, when I had curled up in my shell in some corner somewhere, or in a bathroom, hugging myself and holding my breath as if always trying to return to the state of being a

foetus in its mother's womb. Withdrawing back into my
shell had been exhausting because it drained me of all control over my body. My arms would feel as dry as sticks; my
knees would be like iron rivets; my thighs would be like
saws whose teeth grated at each other. So many days and
hours passed in this way until I found myself shaking and
blinking at the whiteness of the doctor's coat. I still kept my
silence, but it was a different kind of silence now: one containing rest and slumber. The shaking was an effect of
electro-convulsive treatment, the correct term for which I
had never known before I went to Africa. When the doctor
in Beirut asked me, after each collapse, whether they had
given me electro-convulsive treatment in Africa, I finally
understood its significance.

What, now, had become of me? Crying out, lying on
dusty floor tiles in an abandoned building, breathing the
air's fear and sadness, my lord and master a god of death
who had succeeded in making my body tremble with ecstasy for the first time in thirty years. My body had undu-
lated with pleasure as the sniper looked into my eyes. Was
he really the sniper, this person who was now standing up
and who had, for the first time, taken off his trousers? What
had made him into a sniper? Who had given him orders to
kill anonymous passers-by? Would I be thought of as the
sniper's accomplice now my body had become a partner to
his body?

My immediate reaction when I first knew that there was
a sniper lurking on the roof of the apartment block next to
the one where my Aunt Najiba lived was to run trembling
up the stairs two at a time and burst in on our neighbor to
tell her we should contact the radio station or the *Al-Nahar*
newspaper and inform them of the danger. The neighbor
had screamed at me, "Take care you don't breathe such a

thing to another soul! If you do, they'll come and kill us. Anyway, this sniper is most likely acting for the east side." No, I told her, he was killing anyone, irrespective of the side they were on.

The sniper continued to haunt me. In my mind, his image from the first time when I actually saw him, pranced like a hoopoe from one corner of the roof to another, while he made his headquarters next to the water cistern, keeping there a clay pitcher covered by a tin sheet. Even though the hood of his jacket had kept his hair hidden, I had a clear picture of how he looked. I had been hanging out the washing on my Aunt Najiba's balcony, where vine tendrils intertwined with the washing line, when I saw a man on the roof of the neighboring block, carrying a rifle and wearing a hood reminiscent of those of workers in a bakery. He ducked as he ran from one corner to the other, and at once I realized he was one of the militia, then knew he must be the sniper. I stood terrified. A bitten grape I had just popped into my mouth stuck in my throat. I couldn't swallow it or chew it for fear he might notice and kill me.

I knelt, just as he had, and crawled until I reached the door back into the kitchen. I heard my Aunt Najiba say, as she continued lying in bed, "May God grant you strength, Zahra. I hope I live long enough to hang out your children's clothes."

I told her nervously, "Aunt, you must leave tomorrow. You can't stay here any longer. Your hip's better now, but since you must continue to rest, you'd be better off doing it at the village. At least things are safe there."

She searched for an answer, but I went on, "Outside, there's nothing but flying bullets. I can't hang out the washing. I just lay the wet things over chairs." As I said good-bye to her and closed the door behind me, I felt more comfortable, knowing my aunt would not walk outside on to her balcony.

She had hoped that my mother might feel obliged to care for her, after she fell and broke her hip, but my mother refused to take her in. So she had to be transferred to the village, even though she would have preferred to stay on in her room up on the roof, the same room which she had rented when she first came from the south to work in a Beirut sweet factory.

Every time I read about snipers in the news, the image of the sniper came back, prancing from one corner of the roof to the other like a hoopoe hunting for seeds, his binoculars dangling from his neck. He was no longer a fantasy. I tried to wipe the image clean and think how I should act. Should I throw a hand–grenade at him? Should I learn to use a gun and aim it at his heart?

I became obsessed by the sniper, obsessed with noting down the numbers of those killed by him. I began to hold myself responsible for their deaths. I thought constantly of contacting the radio station or the *Al-Nahar* newspaper. But how could I contact them? I didn't even have a telephone.

All these things kept going through my mind even when I was fast asleep, and one day, as I sat and watched the patrons who went into Abu Jamil's restaurant across the road, I sighed. I saw him. I recognized his face, even though his hair was carefully combed so that it flopped forward over his features. I realized I had previously seen it many times in the restaurant before I ever saw it on the roof. Now he sat like any other human being at a table under the awning, brushing the hair away from his eyes. I stood up then, and like a dog with rabies began to roam about the room. I wondered out loud to myself, "What am I to do? I wish Ahmad would come now. Supposing I had a rifle? Yet who would believe me? Who would believe me that this man flicking the hair back from his face, who eats like any other man, who enjoys a dish of *hummus* and *foul,* is the sniper?"

So, for hours, I just sat, addicted to the window. Days passed in this way. Every time I saw the sniper, my thoughts would grow confused, until a strange idea took root in my mind. I wondered what could possibly divert the sniper from aiming his rifle and startle him to the point where he might open his mouth instead? Perhaps a troupe of dancers would do it? Perhaps a gypsy with a performing monkey? Or perhaps a naked woman, passing across his field of fire? Maybe if such a sight crossed his vision he would pause for just one moment and wonder whether the world had indeed gone mad in the midst of this war.

Once, when I saw him again in Abu Jamil's restaurant, I hurriedly found the key to my aunt's room and went straight there, walking from the street of life to the street of death and destruction which the sniper's block, directly next to my aunt's, overshadowed. When I opened the door, I could smell the emptiness. From her room I could see that the neighboring roof was empty. Convinced the man in the café was the sniper, I lay on the bed for an hour or so to await his return. Eventually I stood up and opened the door, frightened I might have made a slight noise. So I waited for a few more moments to be sure that all was quiet. Then I saw that he was leaning against the water cistern, his feet spread out and a clay pitcher at his side. Binoculars dangled around his neck and his hands rested on the rifle, dormant on his hip. He looked as if he slept. I wondered why he chose to stay there on the roof in full view of my aunt's room. Did he imagine it to be no more than a water tank or an attic?

I got undressed and wrapped a towel about my waist. I

twisted another towel around my head and held a third in my hands. Before I could bring myself to show myself thus, I walked about in the room wondering whether such a ruse could work. Then I gathered up my courage and walked out swiftly on to the balcony to face darkness or light, as fate dictated, while humming a current pop song and pretending to hang out the towel on the line. What should I do next? I looked around and could see nothing except the vine, whose grapes had died and dried out, so I could not pull on it and pick them. I became sure that the sniper was loading his rifle without even bothering with his binoculars. I was sure his bullet must cut into my naked back at any moment.

Suddenly I heard myself saying, echoing my mother's tone of voice, "Why can't I cut down these bitches of grapes?" As I turned about as if to go in, perhaps to fetch a knife or shears, my eyes met his as he stood without binoculars, gun or pitcher, a solitary figure next to the water cistern. My heart began to race as I pulled the towel from the line and tried to use it to cover myself. My fingers went to my face in my confusion. But before I could retreat back inside, to my great surprise his calm voice came across to me and asked, "So what is the young lady doing there?"

As I answered, my voice shook. "This room's my aunt's. I come here for a bath as the water's cut off at home."

My answer was an excuse, almost an apology which showed my fear of him. Once I was back inside the room, I felt as if my heart had dropped to the ground and I could no longer breathe. As I got dressed I thought how he had looked like no more than a shy boy from the neighborhood and cursed myself for behaving so insanely. Then, from outside, there a came a rattling sound which froze me as I stood. As I struggled to pull on my shoes, I heard the sound again. Frightened by the noise, I went out and saw two pebbles on the ground and the sniper still where he had been before. His quiet voice carried across to me: "Where do you live?"

I answered, "Opposite Abu Jamil's," my voice like water tumbling in a fountain.

Then he said, "You take quite a risk, coming here."

I nodded agreement, said nothing more. There was a long silence between us before I took my leave and called out, "So long."

He responded, "Go in safety."

As I ran down the stairs I cursed my fear. In the street I held close to the walls. I thought of how one of his bullets could now kill his secret and me with it, even as I also told myself that he couldn't possibly have doubts about me, else why had he let me go? But then I kept wondering when that bullet might hit me and knock me to the ground that was fissured with multicolored craters of many shapes and sizes. A fear that he might not have believed my story overcame me. Perhaps that was why he had asked where I lived. Perhaps he wished to find out which side I was on.

By the time I reached home, which looked deserted from a distance, I found myself hating the sniper for having seen me half-naked and heard me humming a song. Knowing I was alone on the roof, he had brushed me aside, as if I had no importance.

What should I have done, I wondered? I had lost a rare chance, briefly meeting a sniper feared by the community when he was not holding his rifle. I had got him to look at me as a man would look at a woman in peacetime. We had spoken. In spite of that, he had let me go and sent me away, when I should have asked him to lay down his arms. Yet such thoughts soon faded out. All I could do was go back to sitting at the window, observing Abu Jamil's restaurant . . .

And now my cries escaped from my body as I lay in the dust, and before they had a chance to grow any louder I had already called out loudly enough for anyone in the neighborhood to hear. And now the sniper was standing, fastening his trousers and asking in an obvious tone of triumph: "Did I give you pleasure? Did you come?"

I had no answer for him, but kept on staring. For the first time since our relationship began, I started to ask what I was doing here, sprawling in the floor's dirt and dust. What was I here for? Before I came, he would have been picking out his victims' heads as targets, and after I left would be doing the same. Why, every day, did I sneak down that street of death and war and arrive at this place? Could I say I had been able to save anyone, even in those moments when we met and had intercourse? But I couldn't even consider these to hold a reprieve from death for anyone. My visits only replaced his siestas.

I never tried to talk to him on the subject. I couldn't raise any of my former interest in looking at newspapers, or in counting the numbers of his victims. Was I some vulture become human, or had the devil taken human form in me that hot afternoon when my *Qarina* called my name? How did I manage to be so relaxed in this war? My days had beginning and end. I felt secure, even though the rockets still screamed and roared with unabating vigor. I was even able to sleep.

The war had become a perpetual, secure stockade, whose walls were, so to speak, decorated with hearts and arrows drawn in blood. Why had I felt no pleasure before, when I lay on everyday beds? Why had I never clawed at other men's backs as I did at that of this sniper? I wore no make-up, while the war's eruptions seem to have erased those on my own face. Even so, I could not persuade myself I was attractive. Doubtless it was the war and the sniper's lack of contact with life or women which made me the center of his world. Weary, and conscious of bullets not yet fired, I would cry out within myself, never letting him hear my words, "Oh, you sniper! You weigh on me like a vast but weightless mountain! Oh, you who dig these deep craters in my body, can't you dig deeper and deeper until another orifice opens and sets free these old, fearful moments, these images that have until now haunted all my days?"

Oh, sniper, let me cry out in pleasure so that my father hears me and comes to find me sprawled out so. I am one with the dust in this building of death. Let my father see my legs spread wide in submission. Let every part of me submit, from the dark sex between my thighs, to my breasts with their still dormant nipples, my hands able only to tremble.

Here is this god of death who has scorned the loss of my virginity once, twice, a hundred times, the sniper to whom I am grateful for accepting me despite my plainness, because he realizes that beauty is not everything. I hear, close by, scattered gunshots, yet feel as if they are at a great distance. This war has made beauty, money, terror and convention all equally irrelevant. It begins to occur to me that the war, with its miseries and destructiveness, has been necessary for me to start to return to being normal and human.

The war, which makes one expect the worst at any moment, has led me into accepting this new element in my life. Let it happen, let us witness it, let us open ourselves to accept the unknown, no matter what it may bring, disasters or surprises. The war has been essential. It has swept away the hollowness concealed by routines. It has made me ever more alive, ever more tranquil.

My back aches from lying on the ground. I want to rise, but the sniper never seems to have his fill of me. He drops down on me, like a bat out of the air. Yet I like him weighing down on me. I clutch his back so that he weighs as much as possible. It is a weight that transforms itself into lightness until the sniper seems weightless, bodiless.

Yet, as he thrusts into me again and again, I begin to fear that my daily climbing of these stairs must cease. I fear that I may no longer be able to find him. Will our bed have to remain in the dust of death and ruin, and until when? Should I ask him? Why does he not speak more often? He has an affectionate and quiet, even a nervous voice. He seems to sense my fear. No sooner does he hear my footsteps than he looks out to make sure it is me, even though no one else ventures down this street of war. And no sooner have I arrived than the fear dissipates, although remnants of it remain in his tremulous lips and damp hands, and in the wary pupils of his eyes which dart between my face and the space behind me as gunshots echo in the city.

Never once has he told me why he became a sniper. Maybe he thought me illiterate. Yet why, in that case, am I here, exchanging the language of our bodies without previous explanation? My reason for coming to him was that I might put a stop to the sniping. He probably thinks, me being a woman and this a time of war, that I need a man, any man. He must see it as mere chance that the one I have found happens to be a sniper. No other explanation emerges. Never once have I opened my mouth and mentioned his vocation. I said, incidentally, that there were rumors of an armistice, that the war might end soon. He only nodded his head.

Back at home, as if the war had ended for me already, I watered the plants I had been neglecting. I cleaned the mirrors with the newspapers I no longer read. I washed and ironed the cushion covers from the couch. I spread out winter clothes on chairs to get rid of their smell of mothballs. I began to build up stores of provisions, just like my mother before me.

Occasionally Ahmad would make one of his haphazard, unpredictable visits, the effects of hashish clear in his vacant eyes. He would drop down on to the floor, the couch or the mat, whatever was closest to hand. His rifle, beside him, seemingly never fired in anger, would be propped against the table. At first he would subside into a deep slumber, then would rise to forage for food. As we sat and sipped coffee, I would ask him whether newspaper rumors that the war could end shortly were true. Where the sniper had never tried to answer that question, my brother would sigh long and deeply. I could never interpret that sigh. Was it wistfulness or only irritability?

As Ahmad sat and rolled one joint after another, my words could float to him only through that screen of smoke. I would plead with him to stop taking these drugs on which he virtually depended. His response would be: "The whole of Beirut is ours. We, on the western front, and they, our opponents on the eastern front, command between us the buildings and the streets. Nothing that moves or doesn't move is outside our control. We are the force and power and everything! No day passes in which I do not perform an act once prohibited by government or law or mere public opinion. There are other things which I wish to do that are still not approved of, and there is nothing left except drugs. You should praise God that I'm not like those who take a fix of heroin or shoot themselves to pieces."

His yellowed face and blue lips made me withdraw into myself with fear. Then I would ask, "In that case, what's to happen next?" And he would only move his head and sigh that same long, deep sigh. From that point, I would turn over my questions silently in my mind as he dragged on his joint, thought only of himself and faded out of my world.

Perhaps, for him, I also faded out of existence like smoke as I went to fetch more coffee. When I brought the cups back into the room, I needed to watch them to be sure they did not spill; and looked up to see him touching himself. I ran to my bedroom, very distressed. I began to cry, but could not say why I should be so upset. How was it that the war had changed things to this extent: that Ahmad could sit and fondle himself without a thought for my presence as if he were on his own. Oh, war! Why, in coming to my rescue, do you make me reject Ahmad? Yet perhaps he thinks that it is for his own redemption that the war exists, and so he rejects his sister just as she was once rejected by others during the time of peace before the war began. Zahra was the sister of whom Ahmad was ashamed.

Ahmad, what has become of us? Where is our childhood? Where is that photograph of us as children, reaching out, trying to touch the water in the fountain? Where are the sliced lemons that we once squirted into each other's faces until our eyes smarted?

Ahmad, you sit in the next room, fondle your genitals and inhale hashish. You smoke grass and fondle your groin, and can only come back to being yourself after you have killed and robbed, hated and fled. Is it true that you took up arms to defend the rights of the Shi'ites, because they used to say that you and all the Shi'ites were transplanted to Beirut. Or did you use your weapons to defend Palestinians against Phalangists? Or was it the Palestinians who defended you and your cursed luck? Even though I am in the adjoining room, I can still hear your moans of pleasure. Doesn't the fact of this bother you, even as you masturbate? Did Majed and Malek feel as you do as they took their pleasure on my body while it remained as stiff as wood and I sensed a clammy chill in every pore?

Will this war never cease, and if it does, what shall we do then?

"Please don't even start this conversation," Ahmad would say. It was plain to see he was disturbed. Why was he so afraid of the war ending? Because he would then amount to nothing? Overnight, he would become a ghost stalking the streets in which, only the day before, he had been a living presence whose footsteps were heard in the darkness and whose rifle could be used to obtain some bread or a few liters of petrol. After that the gun would lie forgotten in some corner, conveying only memories.

There was no way of engaging Ahmad in conversation, no finding out what the role was which he performed in this war. With each day a new idea came to him, a new thought which he would repeat like a parrot that never stopped mimicking voices. Ahmad came to remind me so much of that pet parrot. One day he would be saying that he was fighting for the Shi'ites and our rights, which were not respected. But perhaps these words were not enough for his comrades or leader, or perhaps he wanted to play up the importance of his role, because he would then add, "I and the others are fighting imperialism; we are fighting America." Another day he would remark, "This is all an Israeli conspiracy to split the Arabs. They want to see us divided, but they'll not succeed." A few days later he might say, "The Palestinians fight with us, but the Palestinians have no right to interfere in what is purely a Lebanese war." And then, a few days after that, he might say, "I, personally, am fighting for the Palestinian cause. All my life I have lived with Palestinians. My friends in the south are Palestinians. Whenever I visited grandfather, I met them and ate their food. My accent became their accent; my dialect their dialect. My sister, I fight for all the under-privileged. I stand with the minorities. It is we, the people of the south, who have been oppressed."

And then Ahmad would reach into the pocket of his dark combat jacket and bring out some newspaper clipping from the *Mouharer,* or one from the *Safir.* He would hand this to me while eating some *kibbé* and continue to speak as the cracked-wheat grains flew all over the table.

"Do you see, sister, how they've turned the whole thing into a sectarian issue? Look at these kids! All they were doing was selling newspapers. For that they killed them! Look! The killed and mutilated are our own people." I would nod in agreement when confronted with Ahmad's very real agitation, as if administering a local anaesthetic to soothe one part of him, even though the effect always wore off quickly.

Sometimes, however, I would ask him whether he ever read newspapers which represented the voices of other warring factions, such as *Al-Amal* or *Ahrar.* "You ought to read the other papers to get a balanced view." At other times I would shake my head and tell him that goods were being stolen indiscriminately. "All sides burn and plunder whatever they can lay hands on, and you are like the rest of them."

He would say, "So you side with the others!"

"Not at all," I would answer.

"Then you side with us?"

I would quickly reply, "No, I never carried a rifle on my shoulder or in my thoughts. I am neutral. I see the pain on both sides."

It is from this apartment and through that window, my only link with the city and the war, and hence with life, that I have seen the trucks drawing up in front of the basement to drop off goods ready for exchange. One evening those "goods" turned out to be men with lowered heads. The guard counted them as if they were beasts for slaughter. And perhaps they did slaughter them, too, for I never saw them emerge again into the street. At times, the more normal goods could form a motley collection: chandeliers, ovens, shoes, medicines and some hair dryers; or juke boxes, sacks of potatoes, foreign neck ties, egg incubators and car spare parts. On one occasion there were hundreds of cackling hens! The stolen goods only leave the basement once a deal has been agreed.

Ahmad had taken to droning on at length, as if talking to himself. "The fighters, whatever side they are on, are thieves. I don't know what to think any more. I believe in carrying arms for many causes, perhaps for all those things I've mentioned, for all the reasons I've stated. Once I was as positive as anyone, but now I'm lost in a dilemma where I wonder about my fighting and its validity, although I do still believe in it. Perhaps it's that I'm trying to escape from myself, never having completed my studies. That's what Zahra has said when we've discussed my justification for bearing arms. But somehow Zahra always tries to throw the whole blame on to me and to nag me over bearing arms, even though she's stopped discussing the subject because it sends her wild, just like she used to be during her nervous fits. When I first came home, she would keep asking the same

question: 'What do you feel when you pull the trigger?'
And I would always reply: 'All I feel when I pull the trigger
is the butt of the rifle knocking me in the shoulder.'

"The war becomes such a wearisome routine that you
have to seek relief from the repetition and boredom. That's
why we use drugs. Drugs have given the war a new dimen-
sion. I can't really explain it. They help you to see the war
through a filter that screens the eyes and shades the trigger.
It cancels out what is seen. It cancels out the comrade who
screamed in anguish before he became still; and our friend
whose guts spilled out beside his new watch. It cancels out
the guns, the rockets, the firing, even though we go on
fighting. And if I ask myself what I have accomplished, I
answer that I have obeyed my commander's orders and
achieved much. I have not stayed at home with the women.
Whenever I hear it said that this war is almost over without
anything being accomplished, I freeze. The end of the war
means I will become a shadow in the streets where, with my
rifle, I have been master, room by room, building by building, tree by tree. I have been master of the nights as well as
of the days.

"Will they make me give back my rifle, or will I be able
to hide it, so that it stays with me? I hope the talk of peace
is only rumor. I don't wish for this war to end. I don't want
to have to worry about what to do next. The war has struc-
tured my days and nights, my financial status, my very self.
It has given me a task that suits me, especially since those
early months when I was so nervous and afraid. Once those
first months were over I became like the cock of the roost,
spreading my rampant feathers. If the war should end without any gain, it will be a terrible loss, a dreadful weakness.
My comrades will have died for nothing. The one whose
guts spilled out will have died for nothing. Everything will

be a lie. Then I shall mourn my comrades, who fell into a trap despite their aspirations."

Ahmad had begun to return with other things apart from his rifle and his joints of hashish. He would try to conceal these objects behind his back as he went across the living room and into our parents' bedroom. Our mother and father were still at the village, constantly pressing me, in messages, to go and stay with them. Ahmad, having entered their room to hide his stolen goods, would come out scratching his stomach. Then he would turn and go back in. I would hear a slight noise. Perhaps he could be changing his hiding place. When he came out he would wear a smile as if bursting with words ready to spill. But as I offered no encouragement he would range about the apartment in a state of frustration. Then he would say something like: "This watch belongs to my friend. He asked me to take care of it for him."

Having got no answer out of me, and perhaps noting my unhappy expression, he would add, scratching his stomach, "It's pure gold, 18-carat. Made in Italy."

He always ended by asking whether I wanted to see it, but I would shake my head in a way that meant he couldn't tell whether I said yes or no.

The second time he brought something back, he couldn't hide it behind him; it was a cassette radio. The third time he carried a silver bird under his arm. By the fourth time he had stopped offering excuses. He was actually rather proud of his acquisitions. "I'm the only one who knows what to take and what to leave behind." He began to show off gold bracelets and rings set with precious stones. The fifth time he held a woman's purse. He went into the bedroom after going to fetch a knife.

The occasion after that he opened up wrappings of newspaper and brought out a yellow dress as bright as the summer sun. "I bought it for you," he announced. And then he came with a round mirror decorated with a transparent, crystal duck. He said proudly, "Just look at this, Zahra. Everyone noticed it but nobody considered taking it. It's not so easy to lift an object like this when you're dodging bombs."

I covered my ears with my hands and screamed, "Stop telling me any of these things!" and took refuge, crying in my room. I heard the refrigerator door open and close: he had forgotten there was no electricity. From the next room, his voice murmured on, saying how the leader of one of the groups had ordered them to stop shooting for fifteen minutes so they could help a doctor's wife who was ready to have her baby any day.

"Her house was like a citadel. As soon as we ceased firing, two of our men got her out. They ran with her to the end of the road, her screams mingling with the clatter of her footsteps as they went towards the spot where her husband waited. After that, it didn't take a moment before the wicked thought occurred to us. The two who had helped her escape had still not returned, and so we headed for the citadel. It seemed as if a treasure cave from *The Thousand and One Nights* had 'opened sesame.' It was exactly as we expected, and here were her many coats, the toys for the expected baby, the ashtrays of silver and others that we thought at first were made of glass, but which turned out to be real crystal. There was yellow brass on the furnishings and the hanging pictures were framed in bronze. We managed to snatch a few small Persian rugs from the walls, and what we couldn't take we smashed. We shot up and stamped on the photographs that stood on the piano. Then somebody said that looting was not enough. Now we must burn the house and destroy the evidence: we should make it seem as if a bomb had scored a direct hit. So here is one of the things I have taken: this mirror with its crystal duck. And I carried it all the way, even though bringing it back has been no easy matter."

Each night, before I went to sleep, I would tip-toe into our parents' room, carrying a candle. There I would survey Ahmad's spoils. I would touch that pure gold pocket watch, made in Italy. And I would read, engraved on it, the name "Samir R," and tremble, just as I trembled once, when the sniper asked me to wear a ring on my finger. Where was Samir R? Did he still live? If so, did he wonder about the fate of his gold watch? I would touch it and ask myself why he should own a pocket watch? Why wasn't it a wrist watch? And I would touch the crystal duck and the reflection which shone from the surface of the mirror in the darkness.

Had the doctor's wife loved ducks so much that she bought one made of crystal on a mirror? If the duck could speak, would it tell me to leave it alone? Would it ask me to set it free, so it could fly back to where it came from? Should I try, tomorrow, to find where Samir R lives and ring him and tell him his gold watch is safe, that I will return it as long as he asks no questions about where I obtained it? Should I search for the doctor's wife and give her back the duck which levitates above its mirror? Might my returning those spoils be considered an abnormal act, comparable to my daily visits to the building of death where its sniper-privateer awaits me?

When I am far away from that freebooter and his vessel, the enormity of the situation becomes more clear. I ask God's forgiveness. What have I done? Got into a love affair with a sniper? And when, each afternoon, my quaking body leads me out on my quest to find him, I tell myself, "Perhaps I'm mistaken in thinking him a sniper. Maybe he's only my aunt's neighbor who likes to watch the war from the roof. His binoculars need be no more than proof of curiosity and need have nothing to do with finding targets for the rifle. Perhaps the poster that says, 'Beware! Sniper,' and the other which reads, 'If you want to be rid of your mother-in-law, get her to pass by here'—perhaps these refer to a sniper in some other building."

Yet didn't I once visit the building after more than a fortnight of truce, and discover he was nowhere to be found? And didn't I, the very first time I went there after the truce was broken, unexpectedly come face to face with him up on the roof? Of course he is a sniper, the freebooter captain of a leaky pirate ship that sails through this war's contradictions and has taken me on board.

Yet I don't want to visit him again, any more than I want to open the door to Ahmad. I would like to chuck all Ahmad's loot off the roof. I just want to stay in this house. If the bathroom had a lock, I would make that my home. But no, I know I will continue to see him every day, to experience that confusion and fear as my feet barely touch the ground or the stair tiles; will know the smell of his sweat, his piercing eyes, my arms gripping his back, making him bear down on me with his full weight. Ah, the beautiful numbness which I feel after I come. For a few moments it plunges me into total darkness. His closed eyes never witness my ecstasy. Yet I myself cannot fully absorb the intensity of those long moments. And when he rises and leaves me lying on the tiles, and turns his tall body away before facing me again, then I forget I have ever promised myself never to return, even as I forget my decision to stop at home and never answer the door.

My one wish is for the war to end so we can make our bed elsewhere. I wish to marry and take this sniper for my husband. I wish to stay with him for ever, but cannot live with him unless we are married. That would be impossible. But I will not give up this relationship, even if he refuses to marry. My father's leather belt no longer holds any fears for me. The war has made it powerless. Neither do I still fear his voice, which has weakened with age, nor his piercing eyes, which now seem covered by moist veils that shift with the constant shaking of his head.

I will not relinquish this relationship. Yet I can only go on living in this apartment so long as my parents stay down south and leave me to my own devices. I can never live with them again. I want to live alone with a man, to tend to his needs each night and morning—if he will marry me. Will he marry me? Should I ask him, "Once the war ends, what will become of us?" Will he believe it is my voice that speaks? The few times I have dared to open my mouth have only been to reply to questions about the things he must have heard in Abu Jamil's restaurant. "Is it true you were married to a rich man in Africa and that he left you because you couldn't bear children? Is it true your brother is fighting with the militia, that you had an affair with someone, and when he married another you became ill and were given electro-convulsive therapy? Is it true you passed your matriculation?"

His words, his lying with me, his standing up again and my watching him as he smokes a cigarette or does up his trousers or touches his face or comments about the *kibbé* I have made, saying, "I'll swear this is the best Shi'ite *kibbé* ever!'' Or his listening for every sound with close attention as he combs his hair without the aid of a mirror. All these details have contradicted the fact of his being a sniper. They reduce that reality to insignificance until it disappears. All his reflexes, seeming so human, put him for me in the category of human being.

No sooner do I return to the house where Ahmad's plunder crouches under my mother's bed, however, than the heaviness of night descends over Beirut, and over all Lebanon. To someone in an airplane drifting in the skies above Lebanon, it must seem as if everything is in order down here. The outlines of homes still stand, trees survive, the moon illumines the nation. But the observer will not be able to see the people shut up behind the walls of their homes, terrified to look over their shoulders, holding their breath out of fear that a missile might detect their presence.

I still, when I think about the sniper, wonder whether he is truly a sniper. Is it necessary for him to kill? Is he insane? And quickly I push away the image of sniper as madman. For, to me, he always seems well-balanced and normally behaved, to show a quiet personality. I've never seen him grow emotional. Perhaps he doesn't need to. There's no dialogue, nothing in common between us, apart from our lying together on the floor.

His features are handsome. His hair drops over his forehead and eyes. His intense eyes show affection, or is that something I only imagine? Tomorrow, when I see him again, I will speak frankly. We will discuss everything concerning sniping and marriage. Tomorrow will decide my future. There's nothing I don't want to know. I'm impatient to know everything. Tomorrow will decide my life.

But as soon as tomorrow arrives the promise I made myself dissolves. My state of mind has changed and I no longer know what it was that bothered me yesterday. My new state seems very different from how I have ever felt in the past. My great need is to sleep. I want to lie in a cool room furnished with only a bed and a bowl of fruit. It was after this mood came over me that, for the first time, as the sniper drew close, I wished he would keep away. As he took me, I felt sleepy, my attention wandered.

It was as if I were lost in fields of lemon trees and green tea. The scents were all mixed up and made my head spin. I surrendered to my dizziness. When I tried to rise, the sniper asked me what was wrong. I told him that when I woke up that morning all I had wanted to do was stay in bed, even though my temperature was practically normal and I felt no discomfort. I heard him say, "Probably you're fatigued." I staggered upright, clutching at the walls.

Since we had already had sex, he sat next to me and offered me a cigarette, having lit one for himself. Our conversation was curious, relating not to us at all but more to distant events far removed from what was going on in the streets below and all over Beirut. He talked of life beyond the mountains. He told me about a barmaid who tried to commit suicide on his account. He described how he fell in love with the daughter of a foreign ambassador when he was sixteen years old, and how he sold his school books for money to take her to the movies. And then how she once caught him with a hose, washing down cars in a car park. The barmaid, he said, had been on the run from the police, having left her job for his sake. Obliged to help her escape, he took her to the mountains, having rented a small room there. He recounted how he lost his virginity, riding with a girl on a camel's back. The girl was so petrified and clung so close to him that he became excited and wouldn't get down from the camel until he had satisfied himself.

I enjoyed these stories in which he relived his adolescence and early manhood. Yet his present and more recent past seemed to be enshrouded in obscurity. I felt incapable of asking about them, even though I was almost suffocating with curiosity. I wanted to know his true name, and what his real feelings were towards me. His manner had never made me feel cheap. In fact, he had always looked happy, waiting for me on the top step. At that instant, my mind went blank, and all I wanted to do was go home and sleep. I wished him good-bye. "Take care of yourself," he told me.

As I went down the stairs I felt unworried, on this occasion, by the sense of eyes peering from behind closed doors on the landings. I had only one thought: "Get home, sleep." When I reached our apartment and saw the door standing open, I called out Ahmad's name. But as I pulled the door shut behind me, I was startled to find my mother standing in the room. She had put on so much weight I hardly recognized her. Her eyes had grown bluer. The southern sun had tanned her face. As she came up to me she lamented, "Alas, alas, Zahra. No word from you. No letter, no greeting. We have been out of our minds with worry, your father and I. What is the reason for it?"

All I could think was, "Oh, dear God . . . How I want to sleep. Why does she have to turn up today? I want to sleep. I am so very tired."

"How does it happen, Zahra, that you keep the house in such a state? The dirt! And no water! Haven't you even been eating?"

But I kept to my one thought: "Where's my bed? I need to sleep. Why does she come today?" And I said, "Mother, I'm feeling unwell. I've caught a chill. I need to sleep a while."

As I headed for my bedroom, she asked, "Where did you

get to? I've been looking all over! If you only knew what I've been through on the journey! I traveled with Dr. Naameh, who said he could only bring me as far as the Hazmieh, and after that I was on my own. I walked the rest. My heart was pounding as if it was wearing wooden clogs. I walked as fast as I could till I got here."

At last I had reached my bed and could lie down. I felt as if someone was lifting me off the bed again. My head went round. Then I felt as if I had been dropped back down on the bed. It was as though I hadn't really moved at all. My hand hurt, the one I had held to my head, and I felt someone standing close to me as my mother's voice asked, "Who do all the things under my bed belong to? I went to sweep out and there they were."

I mumbled, half-asleep, that they were Ahmad's. I wondered why I felt so exhausted. Did I have cancer of the kind which had struck down Soumaya, our neighbor's daughter, my childhood friend, who could never even accept that she was mortally ill? One morning I went to see her. She had been standing on her own two feet in the kitchen, chopping mint and parsley. Her watering eyes dropped a tear as she sliced an onion, just as those would of any healthy woman. She remarked on how pretty she thought my dress. But her belly was swollen. When she saw me looking at it, she laughed and said, "Don't worry. I'm not pregnant. Praise be to God, I already have one boy and two girls, and that's enough. My belly's swollen up because of all those long hours of sitting. God willing, the swelling will go down as soon as I start to get on the move again."

I smiled contentedly. When I told her about an argument I had with my mother when she told me that Soumaya had cancer, she only laughed again, still grasping in her hand a bunch of parsley. "After the results of the tests came," she said, "I was riding with my father in a taxi. He hugged and kissed me and wept. He couldn't stop saying, 'God be thanked, Soumaya, God be thanked. He has taken pity on the husband of yours and those young children!' I didn't understand what he was talking about until he explained: 'I felt sure you hadn't been told what had been said in the report, that the doctor suspected cancer. But, praise God, the results of the test are clear.' "

To begin with, Soumaya went on getting better. But then she went into a decline. Every time I visited her, I saw how blue her complexion was becoming. The navy-blue taint began to spread to her pink lips. Her face shriveled. She continued to eat well, and made plans for finding a house to rent in the suburbs. She and her husband went along together to look at some possibilities, and she spoke about a caftan she wanted to buy and reproached me for not coming to see her more often. She would ask why I didn't take better care of myself, why I didn't try out a new cream for my acne. In the end, I felt that my visits only irritated her. She would keep hold of a small hand mirror and peer into it from time to time, not speaking to me until I was on the verge of leaving.

Even so, she made me promise to visit her each day. She always wanted to go back over our school days and to ask me to tell some of the funny stories about those times we had shared. On one occasion I almost blurted out to her, "You're going to die in a few days. Stop asking such questions. Stop remarking on how pretty this or that dress is. Stop worrying about what you eat or forever carrying a mirror, because you've got to find a way of escaping death."

But then, I thought, perhaps it might be better for Soumaya to be taken by death unawares. I stopped going round there, even though she persisted in sending me daily invitations. Her mother would cry and beat her cheeks and plead with my mother, "Where is your mad Zahra? There's Soumaya on her death bed, asking for her. All she wants is to see Zahra, and Zahra avoids coming. Does not death proceed from God? Or is it disgust that makes Zahra not wish to see Soumaya in this state?"

My mother would burst into my room and cry out, "You heartless wretch with the head of a mule! Go and visit that poor girl!"

In response, I would sit like a sphinx, answering neither her nor anyone, picking my acne. One Sunday I lay in bed, studying the cracks in the walls and the peeling paint and feeling suicidal because I was, for the second time, pregnant by Malek, and due to have an abortion next day at the doctor's clinic where I had it done the first time. As I wondered how I could find the strength to face again the stairs up to that dark threshold, lie on the same table and see, after all was over, the bundle of bloodstained sheets, the door to my bedroom suddenly burst open as though torn apart by a vengeful demon. There my mother stood, beating her forehead and shouting, "Get up! Get up! Say your farewell to Soumaya!"

I couldn't move a muscle. She stepped up to the bed, jerked me by the neck and pounded on my chest, screaming, "You'll send me mad at last, you bastard girl, still dozing in bed! May this be the last sleep you enjoy! Get up! Soumaya lies dying and all you do is sleep!"

Petrified by my mother's sudden attack of madness, I automatically got dressed and went after her, trying to weep but unable to shed a tear. She had put on her black coat. As we went down the stairs, the sound of lamenting echoed up

through every room in the block. Children huddled in the
doorways. I dug my nails into the palms of my hands, trying
to summon the courage to face all these people in distress.

But there was nothing I could have said or done that
would have been appropriate. I sat down on the first empty
chair I came to, close to the bedroom door. Soumaya's father and her three uncles brought out some more chairs for
the women who stood in the doorway, then disappeared
back into the rooms across the hall. Still I wished I could
cry, and still I could not manage it. Those wailing women
had transformed Soumaya's home into an arena of fear and
sorrow. Then Soumaya's mother saw me and came up to
me, a smile distorting her face. "Oh, Zahra, here you are,
come to collect Soumaya on your way to school. She won't
be long. She's almost ready. She's just putting a ribbon in
her hair. Come, Soumaya, Zahra is here for you."

I stood up, but felt like a statue, my face grown rigid with
all my muscles and physical senses. I became as if made of
wood as I confronted the illusion in which Soumaya's
mother strove so hard to believe. She kept on repeating her
words, and the more she spoke the louder the other
women's lamenting became. Two of them propped up Um-
Soumaya on either side as she said, over and over, "Come,
Soumaya, pay attention. Zahra is waiting so you can leave
for school together."

Nothing could shake me out of my pose of a wooden,
silent statue, but Soumaya's mother, managing to slip free
from the grip of the other women, threw herself at me.
With an uncanny strength, she dragged me into Soumaya's
bedroom. My horrified gaze fell on my friend, lying there
and breathing her last. The death-rattle, which seemed to
come from somewhere outside the room, was hers. Her face
had grown longer and narrower, her complexion was blue.

A white kerchief had been tied about her head. Her eyes remained closed, and she seemed deeply asleep, apart from the wheezing in her throat. Two women would now and then lift her head from the pillow to offer her some drops of water. To my tremulous surprise, she opened her lips and drank each time. But then I burst into hysterics as I saw her green dress laid out next to the bed, as if ready for her to put on, and saw her slippers, so familiar to me, laid on the floor by the bed, waiting for her to place her feet in them . . .

So was it now my fate to be stricken with cancer too? My mother had arrived from the south as if some inner voice had summoned her to be at my side, to offer me water, to tie a kerchief about my head. And even at that moment, Ahmad's loot lay under the bed as if testifying how its very presence was bringing about the death of the household's daughter.

I lay there paralyzed. Was it because I was still asleep? I found that I kept staring towards the window, as if anticipating that the sniper might appear in it at any moment and claim I had agreed he could have sex with me as soon as it was closed behind him. But it was only a dream into which my mother's voice broke next morning and roused me from the bed. In no time, I began to feel a little better; the sensations of dizziness and sickness subsided. At lunchtime, there was an odor of cumin. My mother was cooking tomato *kibbé*. I ate it without bread or spoon, and as I ate my mother said, "There's why you're sick. You haven't been eating properly."

"It was because I was sick that I wanted to lie down and not eat. I just needed that to make me feel better. I never know whether Ahmad will turn up from one day to the next. Stop making so much fuss. I'm off out now. I've been getting out each afternoon to visit a friend, this girl I got to know last month. We've been calling on each other, and there's not so much bombing in the afternoons. There's no sniper, so don't concern yourself. And don't yell at me. I'm going anyway!"

The street was practically deserted, but I ducked as I went, fearful of hearing shooting. I almost ran, wondering how I would ever reach the building without being shot; wondering at the way I daily promised myself that today would be the one on which I brought up the subject of marriage. Our relationship had certainly been developing, but no sooner did I arrive than I fell mute. I couldn't wait for the moment when he drew me on to the ground, for the moments which blotted out the sounds of war.

Was the street always how I now saw it: empty except for one old man carrying a bag, the barricade, a clutch of young militia and the pall of flavorless dust that hovered above its shuttered shop fronts, the voices of children sounding from inside, but outside a silence all-commanding over even the trees and lamp standards? How did I manage to walk this street each day with no one stopping me, no one challenging me? But about halfway along the silence became awesome. Did everyone know I was on my way to visit the one who ruled here? Was this why they let me pass like the Queen of Sheba amid their disquieted stares? As soon as I had reached the base of the sniper's building, I felt amazed that no one had shot me. I had slipped through the nets of a hundred hunters, passed through a circus's row of fiery hoops. As I mounted the flights of stairs they seemed to stretch up for ever, as if they might take me as far as outer space and bring me face to face with a wall of fire.

By the time I reached the top flight I was trembling with exhaustion, hunger and thirst, even though I had eaten and

drunk only a short while before. A few more steps took me
to where he waited, smiling. As he covered me with his
body as usual, I felt in my stomach a rising and falling of
nausea.

I reached for a tissue which lay beside the sheets he had
bought a month before to improve our makeshift bed. I
didn't want to get any vomit on the sheets and rushed to
the stairs. As I began to throw up, I felt like death. I heard
him say, "Take these tissues," but I waved him away with
my hand. Yet where could he have gone to? He turned his
back. I raised myself, reached for the box of tissues and tried
to clean up the mess. Then I went to the pitcher and rinsed
my hands and mouth with water. I heard him say, "It's all
right, you're sick. If it doesn't improve you'd better see a
doctor close to home. Perhaps he can give you something
for your stomach."

But I shook my head, smelling the stench of vomit. Then
I asked, "Do you actually live in this building?"

Perhaps I took him by surprise, maybe not. There was no
reaction in his face. He answered me in his level tone of
voice, "Yes. So what?"

And I said, "Couldn't you fetch a mop so I can clean this
up?"

Perhaps he was satisfied with my reason for asking
whether he lived there, maybe not. He only said, "Don't
worry. I'll clean up later."

At this point we could have started a conversation or begun to talk about what was on my mind, using the episode
as the pretext. Instead, he told me lie after lie. His family,
he said, still lived on one of the floors of the block, and he
didn't feel he needed to explain why he had never introduced me in his home. Explanations were quite unneces-
sary. On this street, no girl entered a young man's home

while his parents were present, and that was why we had to meet on the stairs. His answer stopped my hopes in their tracks. I felt he had destroyed all our lines of communication. It was as if the hours we had spent together and our physical intimacy had never given him the chance to be honest! Where, now, were the dreams I had had at home that he would ask me to marry him when the war ended? Perhaps he felt that we could meet only in this way. Perhaps the truth was that he would slip from my view as soon as the bullets ceased and the rockets stopped, and that I would be left with only my shell to retreat into.

But no, no! I cannot let it happen! I will not accept that these gulfs can never be bridged. My body's secrets have been laid bare, and if the sniper, who has told me his name is Sami—though secretly I believe this to be false—if the sniper should leave me, there can be no other man in my life or for my body.

The war has swept everything away, for the rich and for the poor, for the beautiful and for the ugly. It has kneaded everything together into a common dough. My own looks have altered. I am no longer bothered by pimples on my neck, where once I felt that these were an inevitable part of me and that I and they could never part company. Now, as I lie in bed, I look at the print of a Persian woman hanging next to the wardrobe, a picture with which I grew up. Whenever I used to look at it, I would grow even more firmly convinced that I was a very different breed from such a woman. She was a creature of legend: beautiful, with a beauty that dazzled. Yet when, now, I lie in bed, it seems that I have joined that species of woman and am able to bear a comparison with her.

Yet why was my giddiness making it so difficult for me to lie down; so hard to grip my toothbrush; so hard to lift a

cup and drink its contents? My appetite had gone completely. From time to time my mother came in to offer me a
bowl of soup and to cover me up and make me sweat. This
would, she assured me, make me feel better. "You seem like
a pregnant woman. Like a Bedouin who has just aborted,"
she remarked.

I only smiled and thought how those days when I became
pregnant and needed to undergo abortions were gone for
ever. The old doctor and the nurse were gone, their
wooden table with them. Their building had been destroyed. Why had I been so afraid to buy birth-control pills?
Did the pharmacist frighten me? Was I more afraid of him
than of needing an abortion?

It was always my fear of people which put me into a
pathetic state, but that fear had evaporated with the war to a
point where I was able to look the pharmacist in the face
and ask for ten packs of contraceptive tablets. The look he
gave me made me waver, but I summoned my resolve and
told him I really did need ten packs. His expression almost
undermined my courage, but at last he said, "Ten packs is a
great many, madame. We are in the middle of a war. You
should give others a chance, too. Why not just take five?"

But I insisted and paid and held the pills close to me as I
left. I would no longer be such a fool as I had been in the
past, and this would be a private matter, kept safe inside my
thoughts. That was why I picked a pharmacy far from home
in which to buy them.

I took two pills at once, to guard against our love-making
of only three days before, and after that followed the instructions on the package carefully. When I woke up one
morning in a pool of blood, it occurred to me that the pills
were making my period extra heavy. By the time I started
on the second pack, I was taking a pill every night. My

hiding place was one of Ahmad's woollen socks. Before I
was through the second pack, I had once more swum in a
sea of blood.

I kept meticulously to the instructions. But during the
third month, as I impatiently awaited my period, there was
no sign of it. The instructions said, however, that it could
be delayed. I only needed to count up to five days, as if my
period had happened, and then resume the pills. I began a
new pack in the fourth month. But when, once more, I
awaited my period in vain, I almost prayed that I might be
immersed in that sea of blood. All to no avail. I decided to
wait one more week and then see a doctor, though which
doctor would I dare to visit? Perhaps the best idea would be
to go to the Makasid Hospital near-by. It had many doctors
and no one there knew me. Should I choose that hospital or
another? I was uncertain. Every hospital had a casualty unit
to take care of the wounded in these times of danger. Perhaps I should put off going a bit longer. Perhaps it was the
blood trapped in my body that was making me feel giddy
and nauseated.

This was certainly how I felt when taking the pills, especially after I got up each morning. Perhaps the streams of
trapped blood had turned toxic inside me. It seemed impossible! I had to see a doctor! Should I tell the sniper? Or wait
until after I had seen a doctor? There was no way out. My
situation was growing worse. I kept feeling nauseated and
wanting to vomit, but couldn't swallow one drop of water.
As I grew paler I became sure that something was terribly
wrong. Perhaps I had liver damage. My eyes were yellowish
and I suffered from a constant headache, concentrated above
my right eye and beating inside the vein that linked my eye
and forehead. The headache turned me into a pharaoh's
statue, unmoving for fear of pain.

Ahmad arrived at noon, and I heard my mother opening the door to him and her bewailings growing louder as they stood outside my bedroom. Ahmad, carrying his Kalashnikov rifle, had handed her a package, telling her to prepare calves' liver. But then he asked with concern: "What? Zahra sick? There are all sorts of bugs about these days! It sounds like her stomach's infected. I'll fetch a doctor, any doctor you ask for. With this gun stuck in his back he'll come like a robot." Then he began to laugh and added, "You know, two days ago Nadim Zaatar was wounded. We took him to the American Hospital and stuck a Kalashnikov in the back of the doctor who said he needed a critical operation. We don't understand all your talk, we said, but if this young fellow doesn't live, you'll be shot as well. And because of our threats, Nadim Zaatar's alive today!"

I wanted to shut my ears to Ahmad's words. His voice irritated me. The brutality in his laugh irritated me. Everything about him irritated me. As my headache grew worse, I closed my eyes. My headache, at least, was mine alone. After some more time had passed, I called out to my mother, but seemed to be alone in the apartment. I looked at my watch. It was about four o'clock. I was going to be late for our assignation. I dressed like a madwoman.

The energy it had cost me to reach the sniper's hideout was only too obvious. For the first time in any of our meetings I tugged on my skirt hem to stop him from lifting it, even though he had already drawn me down on the floor. Sensing that something was wrong, he asked, slightly disappointed, "Are you still unwell? Why did you come, in that case? You should have rested today." Then he added, "I see your belly's swelling. Watch it! You could be pregnant."

His voice sounded matter-of-fact, with no tone of anger in it, and I felt relieved he had shown no annoyance or

disturbance. I simply said, "I'm afraid I may have cancer. I
had a friend who got cancer, and her stomach swelled up."

I could not judge the effect my words had on him, because I spoke them as though I were confessing them to
myself, to the surrounding walls, to the silence on the stairways. I only wished I could stand up as I used to, and feel
healthy. I wondered whether those days would ever return.

Why had I got into this state? What had made me ill?
Why had my sickness not allowed me to slip through its
fingers like water, and float away free? Why had it tightened
its grip on me? Men and women continued to be healthy
only because there was no time now for being sick, only
time for bullets. Or had God chosen me so that the fighters
might realize there is such a thing as natural pain and death;
and did Ahmad know how, when I told my mother the
comedian Shoushou had died from natural causes, she became relaxed and happy, as if I had denied the news of his
death altogether?

Any illness nowadays must be fraught with danger. The
doctor who examines you is likely to shout, "We've no time
for illness!" The nurse, who should be helping you to stand,
is likely to pull her shoulder away from under your hand
and say, "We've no time to give you."

I entered the doors of the Makasid Hospital and walked
into its white corridors. A number of women were lying
around in white, and young men and women in combat
uniform were drifting about. I left and, coming to a store,
asked for a telephone directory. After searching for the
name of a physician I finally found, under the heading "Gy-
necologists," someone with an address in the Mazraa district. As luck would have it, the man himself answered and
suggested I come to his clinic straight away.

I went out into the drizzle. As it began to come down

harder and to soak me to the skin, I flagged down a cab and gave the driver the address. He said he could only take me if I paid five liras. When I gasped at the fare, he mimicked my shock and said, "Where have you been living, lady? Petrol costs me a hundred liras, and I only wish it were decent quality. And I have to steer this cab through dangerous times."

I thought to myself, "So what is so dangerous about them?" If I decide to ignore the war, there's nothing to prove its existence as the rain falls and people scurry past. The stores are open, and lingerie hangs on display in one of their doorways. You can get *shish kabab* and *shawarma* everywhere, and *falafel* goes on being produced by the hundred. It is only the explosions, close by or in the distance, which disturb the normality of life.

The building where the gynecologist had his clinic was strange. The approach to it lay through an abandoned garden. On the first landing I came to a door, but couldn't make out which floor I needed. When I knocked on the door no one opened it, but an old woman's voice asked, "Who do you want?"

I replied, "Dr. Razak."

The old voice answered, "Upstairs."

I climbed the stairs and arrived breathless at the end of a corridor. A young girl answered my knock, and when I asked for the doctor, she called out, "There's a woman here asking for you, Baba."

The doctor came to the door, his hand held out in greeting, and asked that I should follow. I couldn't avoid a suspicion that he was not a real doctor. There was something very odd about the place. Various boys, aged between five and ten, were dressed in white nightgowns, some sitting, some jumping about, others crying. One of them had his

mother with him. The doctor led me to a side-room, where
a fifteen-year-old groaned, spread out on a table, as a mid-
dle-aged woman, who must have been his mother, wiped
his hair and forehead. She was saying to him, "Don't worry,
my love. You have finished with this agony."

The doctor turned to her and said, "Now, be careful. As
I told you, no movement, no bathing, no underwear. Do
you have a nightgown? You can buy the one he's wearing."

The woman asked the price, and the doctor said jumpily,
"Give me whatever you can afford; three liras will do."

She reached inside her bodice and brought out a knotted
handkerchief. As she undid the knot, the doctor impatiently
snapped his fingers at her to get her to hurry. And after he
had taken the two liras she offered, he didn't comment but
went to the table to give the youth a hand up, saying,
"Come now, be a man," as the mother tried to help to raise
him from the other side.

But the boy moaned each time they tried to raise him,
and when his moans became a scream, the doctor said nervously, "Wait, I'll get someone to help you carry the lad.
You can pay him a few piastres." He didn't even give her a
chance to reply before shouting, "Concierge! Here! You're
needed."

I stood and watched in astonishment. Could this man
who performed circumcisions also be a women's specialist?
Perhaps I had misread the heading. If so, why had he offered
me an appointment and allowed me into his clinic?

The concierge arrived with, in his wake, a very heavy
woman who bellowed, "Look here, doctor! Why do you
keep interfering in things which concern the kitchen and
food? If you're worried about this tripe, you can clean it
and cook it yourself!"

The doctor didn't reply, but flapped his hand agitatedly

back and forth as he said to the concierge, "Come on now, please! Carry this boy. His mother will give you a few piastres."

The concierge went up to the boy and picked him up as if he had been a young child.

The mother asked, "Doctor, should we come back in a week's time?"

Taking a sheet from his drawer, the doctor nodded. "Just do as I told you. No bathing, no playing, no underwear."

He laid the fresh sheet on the table and, without looking at me, asked what my problem was. Before I had a chance to answer he had left me, sticking his head out of the door and yelling, "Be patient! Don't go away! I just have to examine this woman. It'll only take five minutes."

Then he shut the door and turned to me, his large nose projecting like a mountain between the oval lenses of his glasses. "So what's your problem?" he asked again nervously. I told him. Then, as if he had not heard a word and without asking a single further question, he pointed to the table and said, "Take off your pants and cover yourself with the sheet."

As he drew a curtain across the room, I took off my knickers, but didn't know where to put them. I pushed them into the yellow plastic bag.

I lay back on the table, eyes gazing at the ceiling as the doctor put his hand under the sheet. As he tried to make his examination, I stiffened. I heard him say, "Come now! You let your husband sleep with you, and now you're frightened of my finger! Come now! Stop being so foolish, sister!"

I tried to relax, but couldn't. I tried to open my thighs, but couldn't. I tried to control the contractions in my lower abdomen, but couldn't.

I heard him say again, "Come, sister. What's the prob-

lem? Are we playing games? Look, I'm a busy man! I have
ten more boys to circumcise before dark."

The more I tried to relax, the more tense it made me. He
took off his glasses, threw them down on the table and said,
"OK, lady, get your clothes on and go in peace." When I
begged him to try just once more, he scowled at me before
placing one hand on my abdomen as the other explored
inside. Then he said, "Congratulations. You're about four
months pregnant." Lifting the sheet to my waist, he added,
"You should have known that without me. Your waistline's
gone and your belly's big. It'll cost you ten liras for the
examination."

I cried out, "But I can't be pregnant. I've been getting
my period each month except for the last two months."

He looked at me furiously and said, "Look, young lady,
I've been in practice thirty-five years, performing circumcisions, delivering babies. I can tell what a woman is carrying
at the first examination. So what fairy stories do you want
to tell me? Come on, lady. I've ten young lads waiting to be
circumcised and I need to give them examinations."

I asked incredulously, "So what were my monthly peri-
ods?"

"It must have been blood from a hemorrhage, lady. It
certainly wasn't from any period."

"But I took the pills!" I cried. "Can you get pregnant
when you're on the pill?"

"You were probably pregnant before you started taking
them. Probably by a week, or even a couple of days. Maybe
the pills gave you a hemorrhage. At any rate, you're pregnant now, so stop your chatter and pay up the ten liras for
this examination. Come and see me again when you're
eight months pregnant. For the time being, I'll prescribe
you some vitamins."

He began to write on a piece of paper, but I was almost beside myself and cried out, "Doctor, I don't want to have this child. Please give me an abortion at once!"

He showed no surprise at my words, but went on writing the prescription, which he then folded and held out to me. Instead of taking it, I began to plead, "I beg you. I'm in your hands. I implore you. Give me an abortion now."

"Women never believe they're pregnant," he mused. "First they can't wait to be pregnant, and then, when it happens, they go all coy and say, 'I really didn't want this to happen.'" Then he yelled at me, "Woman, are you educated or are you ignorant? How can I possibly give you an abortion when you're four months into your pregnancy? If it were one, two or three months, that would be fine. I could close the door and, in five minutes, perform an abortion. But now it's impossible. You're bearing life."

I pleaded, "Give me something to poison the child."

For a moment he stayed silent. "My word, you are a stubborn and ignorant one," he laughed in the end. "Don't you know that whatever you take will poison and kill you first before it poisons and kills the child?"

"But I want a divorce from my husband," I cried. "He's in love with someone else."

"In that case, the law's on your side," he responded. "He'll be obliged to give you a pension, alimony and child-care allowance, since you became pregnant before the divorce. It's much better that you should have found out before getting divorced."

My head started to throb, my heart to pound. I clutched at my thighs with my fingernails and cried out, "My husband's been in the fighting and is dead. Why do you stand in my way and ruin my life? I beg you, doctor, implore you. I'll give you 500 liras, 800 liras."

My head throbbed, my heart pounded, my nails dug into
my thighs and I shook all over. The doctor rose from behind his desk and stood before me. He cupped my face in
his hands and he said, almost in a whisper, "Listen, woman,
and listen well. You've been pregnant for four months.
You're already into your fifth. It isn't possible for you to
have an abortion. No one in the world would give you an
abortion, not even if the prophet Mohammed or Jesus were
to say so. If God wore a doctor's gown, he'd refuse you an
abortion. It would place your life in jeopardy. If you offered
me 1,000 or 100,000 liras, I still wouldn't touch you. Now
do you understand? May God grant you patience and so-
lace."

As he turned from me I looked desperately around. My
eyes became fixed on the door and I thought perhaps I'd
refuse to leave until there was a solution. But then I thought
that the only solution was suicide: there could be no alter-
native to that, once I had left his office. I opened my purse
and gave him a fifty-lira note. He took it, turning it over
and running it through his fingers. His nose still jutted out,
like a mountain, from under his spectacles. He counted out
the change, as if he were a merchant completing a sale. I
stated aloud to myself, to my mother, to the sniper, to the
whole world, "I'll kill myself if I can't get an abortion."

He raised his head, pursed his lips mockingly and winked
an eye. "Very smart!"

This calmed me down, and I said, "Doctor, I'm frightened I may have cancer. I'm sure I'm not pregnant."

Having pushed the change for the fifty liras towards me,
he stood up. "Maybe God has sent us another Virgin Mary
unawares. Get yourself some X-rays done at the Makasid
Hospital. I'll write you a note so you can go there, though

it's a pity to throw away good money. You're nothing more than pregnant."

Before I could fly out of control again and answer him, the door reopened and the heavy woman came back in. Although I was feeling lost in the middle of a pit of fear, there was something about the whiteness of her full, round face in contrast to her dyed black hair that caught my attention. There she stood, her hand on her hip, looking from me to the doctor and back. She said, "This examination seems to be never-ending." Then, letting one hand drop and raising the other to her waist, she added, "Those kids outside have turned the place upside down. What do you want we should do? Shall I tell them the doctor's still busy, still examining, or what?"

The doctor went to the door, glanced back at me and said, "Come now, sister. God grant you patience."

That woman's looks had frightened me. I went down the stairs, the terror of what I must face freezing my concentration. I drifted through the streets. The rain had passed over, but left in its wake was a rainbow, which made me think, "Look how the rainbow still fulfills its role, despite the sounds of fear in the city." My own fear seemed to have deadened the sounds of explosions. I hadn't noticed how the streets were empty except for militia.

"Stop, woman! What are you doing out, still on the streets?"

Without showing much concern, I answered, "I've been to visit my mother in hospital." I continued to walk without paying any heed to their advice that I should walk quickly, as fast as I was able. Hurry? Protect myself? What need did I have to protect myself when I was planning to end my life anyway? Why did my mother have to come from the south just now, when the easiest thing would have been for me to swallow a bottleful of aspirin and lie down on the bed to die? To myself I kept repeating, "Aspro's my friend. Aspro's my companion. Aspro relieves my pain and suffering," just as the advertisements put it. But I could not remember how the advertisement went at the end. I had read somewhere that the repetition of a particular sentence helps with forgetting the present and moving on as the poison takes effect.

I imagined the sniper watching out next day for the yellow plastic bag, anticipating my footsteps on the stairs, but seeing and hearing nothing. His box of tissues would remain full, the sheet unruffled. As the rifle and binoculars still leaned in their corner, the water pitcher would stay undisturbed. But, at home, my mother's screams would ring out as if they were ripped from her throat. Fear on the verge of hysteria would distort her face, her hands make wild gestures in the air. I wondered whether she would think of the past, and of my existence as an extension of her own since we had been inseparable, like orange and navel. Perhaps I was now the only link she had with her youth, and once I was dead, everything would have gone with me. Would Ahmad weep? Do a man's tears fall easily? If he heard of my death while carrying his loot, would he conceal it before deciding to weep? Or would he cover his face instantly and let his stolen goods drop to the ground? In their falling, perhaps they would break. Would someone then come and sweep up the pieces? With Zahra laid out on the bed, nothing on earth would be important. Would our house be filled only with women, or would there be one room set aside for women, another for men? Or would the war sanction a mingling of the sexes? Poor Zahra, what a wasted youth.

Why did you end it like this? Come, Zahra, time to get up. Time to go to school with Soumaya. But Soumaya already lies with the dust, so my mother cannot say this as she sees Soumaya's mother enter. Instead she will say, "Zahra has gone after Soumaya and perhaps, when they meet, they will go on together to school."

The girls' school at Bourj Abu Haidar: "Zahra, why haven't you starched your collar? Who embroidered this cedar on it? Can it be there is someone who doesn't know how to embroider the cedar? Who picked out the colors, this faded green? Show me your finger nails. Why is this one so long? Crooked, yes, but why so long? The doctor told you not to cut your nails? Show me your head. Let me see. Are these spots dandruff or lice? My God! These are lice! Have you been up to the village? Show me your hands. What have you got on them? Henna? Henna on your hands? Tell your mother to get rid of this henna. You're attending school, not the market place among pedlars. Your hands are still stained reddish yellow. Why don't you scrub them? What do I hear? You can't wash off henna? It only goes away with time? That means we must wait a whole year for it to disappear. I never heard such a thing. Ah, but Zahra's a good student, the best in school. She gets high grades—in history, a hundred per cent; in geography, a hundred per cent; in composition and for her essay 'And Paradise Lies under the Mother's Feet' . . . What? She's handed in an empty sheet? What's up with you, Zahra? Very well, you can go home. You're sick? You have a stomach ache? Very well. We'll send Sadia with you."

Sadia is wife to the school janitor. She holds my hand as we cross the street. As she talks, she slanders all the girls in the schools. "Every one of them is a whore." I don't understand the word she uses. "That cursed Najwa has had my husband put in jail. She swore he slept with her, but we all know she lost her maidenhead at the time of the Flood."

Thank God I'm no longer at school. Thank God the time is so out of joint, both in Beirut and at home, that no one notices my swelling belly. Yet won't it show when I'm laid out on my back? Won't they send for the doctor then? If my mother's alone in the apartment, will she unrape me? In her hysteria, will she try to summon me back to life? Will she observe how my waist has disappeared, how the color of my nipples has changed? Will she notice how my stomach has distended? No, my mother will cover me up again; she will not call in the doctor to give an opinion and ensure that there is a scandal. But my father will drive her into the kitchen and beat her, feeble as he is, with his leather belt. He will say, "Like mother, like daughter. No matter how hard you try to make things otherwise, the daughter will still follow her mother's example. You're to blame, you bitch. You sold your honor and your daughter's with it. Who got her pregnant? You tell me that! Why couldn't you go to your lover on your own? Why did you always have to take her along as witness? That poor, inno-cent, wretched creature? From car to car; from Damascus to Beirut; from Sofar to the south. Tell me, who was it who got her pregnant? You're no *hajja*. You're a bitch."

Had my father found out about Malek at the time, he would have leapt on me, however frail and still I may have been as I lay on the bed. Now, I think all he could do would be to shake his head from left to right, feeling sorry he hadn't beaten me enough when he was still strong, like a lion in his own stretch of jungle, growling out his words and devouring whatever crossed his path. He would shake his head and mutter to himself, "Dear God, to think of Zahra, the best girl in school. Zahra, the reasonable, quiet, affectionate girl, who traveled from home to school and back, from home to work, never looking to left or right, never staying out late. When she had her first period, she locked herself in the bathroom for two hours till her mother knocked on the door and said, 'My dear Zahra, have no fear. This is God's will. Open the door and don't be silly. Just open the door, now. Very well, I'll stay outside, but open the door. It's nothing of which to be afraid.' Thus Zahra joined the circle of women. And now may God send her mother into perdition a hundred times. May God curse her mother, and curse all her guilty offspring. Ahmad's a rascal and thief; Zahra's a little bitch. And the big bitch wears a black veil and coat and heavy stockings."

"What am I to do?" I asked myself as I continued walking. My footsteps echoed, but my ears were deaf and registered no sound. If I were to kill myself, then everyone would know I had been pregnant. But by the time they found out, I would be laid out for ever—I, and whoever was in my stomach, ready to travel underground into total silence. Above us, the noise, the din and the fighting would continue between cease-fires. The conventions would continue, marriage would continue, giving birth would continue. And the houses, the rain and sun would all remain. Everything in turmoil; everyone inevitably moving towards the moment when they, too, must be laid out. All became equal in that moment. It must be the same for everyone in the end. But my moment will be the more difficult because I am the one who has decided upon and prepared for it.

As I arrived home I could hear my mother screeching. Had she begun to mourn and prepare for my funeral already, before I had even swallowed the white pills, each one looking exactly like the next? Was she trying to tell me that she knew what I had it in mind to do and was trying to stop me with a display of hysteria? Perhaps she would change her ideas about dissuading me once she saw my body, waist, belly and nipples; and after I'd told her what the doctor had said: "Look, sister, you've been pregnant four months and you're already into your fifth. You can't have an abortion. No one in the world would give you an abortion, even if the prophet Mohammed or Jesus were to say so. If God wore a doctor's gown, he'd refuse you an abortion. It would place your life in jeopardy. If you offered me 100,000 liras, I still wouldn't touch you. Do you understand, woman? May God grant you strength."

I wished to be rid of this foetus. It created a throbbing in my head and made me nauseated and dreadfully tired all the time. It made me think that cancer had struck at my belly. Or was this a cancer in the guise of a foetus?

I wondered how my mother would react if I were to tell her. Would she beat me? Very good. Would she bite me as she used to when she really went wild? Even better. Every possibility has been covered. But I do not want her to escape the burden of this pregnancy. I want to be able to lie down soon after I tell her, instead of having to grit my teeth. Let her spin round in circles until she goes mad, then I'll lie down.

Just once I want that special fear to creep up on her—the fear that is not like the one set off by explosions and flying bullets. I want her to feel my fear in the way that she made me feel her anxiety as we stood together in that darkened room. I want her to feel my fear and to tremble. I want her to wet herself, awake or asleep. I want to see her having to carry her mattress up on to the roof, where the neighbors will notice her and laugh and whisper, "See, she can no longer hold her urine."

All those occasions when she made me watch out for people who might be known to us. "Come now, Zahra. Come now, be a dear. If you see someone we know, just bend your head and tell me . . . Listen, Zahra, we've been to the doctor's. We had to go to the doctor's." But the walls on the way to Dr. Shawky's would have been splattered by the mulberry fruit that the bat stole. The wall we passed had been whitewashed. "Well, perhaps they whitewashed it while we were in the doctor's." But the doctor's room is different. The table is different. The wall there has a picture of a child in an advertisement for some special kind of milk, and another picture of a blond baby snuggling into its mother's breast.

The bed where we went is different, the pattern on the floor different. "We went to the doctor's. Do you understand?" But the doctor's face is different. He doesn't close the shutters and make the room dark. From the doctor's windows you can see the great mulberry tree and its leaves. That other room was always dark. The darkness makes it impossible to see any pictures on the wall, except for the portrait of a frowning man in military outfit, showing off his medals and decorations . . .

"Where did you get to? How you've frightened me. My God, my daughter is unhinged!" Then my mother turned to our neighbor and asked, "What right does this hussy have to slip out of the house while I go to borrow some cardamom. She goes just like that, and then is gone three hours! It's disgraceful. The world's upside down. Tell me, where have you been?"

And our neighbor, Altaf, answered on my behalf, *"Hajja,* you can be sure she visited the communists. She's been practicing how to fire a Kalashnikov. While you were away all the young women went to the Communist HQ to sign on, each according to her ability. A strong one can carry arms, the awkward ones cook for them, and those with 'other talents,' well . . . need I say more?"

My mother stared at me, perhaps trying to work out into which category I fitted. I was still wet from the rain and the droplets ran down my face and clothes and fell on to the floor. I must have looked a sight. My mother tried to conceal a smile, but then she caught our neighbor's eye and they burst out laughing together. "Well, did you ever!" they said in unison, and their laughter grew. As my mother mopped at the tears of her laughter, so I dried my own tears which had no wish to fall. The tears brimming in my eyes came from deep inside, from a soul bursting with hatred. They saw me as a laughing stock. Our neighbor, Altaf, saw me as a laughing stock, and my mother showed her agreement. The idea that she might take any responsibility for my problems seemed too remote. All she will do is laugh and say, "It's beyond belief that any man would want to come near you. I can't imagine you in relation to any man."

When I came back from Africa the first time, she had never stopped asking me whether my real reason for hating Majed went back to my hating what happens between a man and a woman. I never commented but kept my silence. Her questions never stopped, but I ignored them until, at last, I burst out, "He slept with me. That's nothing to do with it!"

And she cried out, "Dear God, I don't believe it! If I saw it with my own eyes, I couldn't believe it."

Two days later, she broached the subject again in a different way by offering some advice: how I ought to play the coquette, be flirtatious and coy. How I ought to run up to my husband the minute he came in at the door and kiss him on the cheek. How I ought to take a bath each evening, and every night wear a different gown and spray cologne on my body; and maybe put a flower in my hair and stop going barefoot, while never answering him back in a loud voice. Her words were enough to make me hate Majed more than I did already, and to hate having to live with her in Lebanon. Now she was laughing at me openly.

It seemed, at this point, as though my relationship with the sniper had become no more than another aspect of the war. It seemed as though his lying on top of me had no meaning, as though I had never held him close, wanting him to press his full weight down on me. It was as though I had never cried out with pleasure, as though I had felt no ecstasy but had remained motionless beneath him.

Now he seems to stand outside the frame of the moving picture of my imagination, even though I can say he's the reason for my present problem. Nevertheless he does not find his way back into my thoughts. My mind is blank where he is concerned. Can that be because I think I can anticipate what his reaction will be when he hears I am pregnant by him? "My God, Zahra. You must get an abortion!" It comes back to me how, in those circumstances, Malek would seem to age, his face grow long and pale as though he were the one carrying a baby.

But with Malek it was a different situation. He was married, whereas my sniper is still a bachelor, is he not? All the chaos and anarchy in Beirut will surely make it seem to him that Zahra should go through with her pregnancy and bear the child once they have been married in a speedily held wedding. Such thoughts kept pressing through my head. For the first time, the whole problem of my pregnancy seemed to grow simple. The sniper who said his name was Sami entered into every thought, creating images of happiness as I remembered how he would look at me, long and slow, his

204   *Hanan al-Shaykh*

courteous manners, his body pressed to mine, his anticipating my arrival day after day. The stream of memories and
stories that he told about his youth never ran dry. He had
opened his heart to me, even though he still spoke only of
the past. And why should that not be so? If he didn't want
to mention his present, then it must be because he thought I
already knew all about it. Or perhaps he feared that, if I
knew more, it might make me want to stop seeing him.
Suppose I were to tell him everything I felt. Perhaps his fear
would disperse then, and the problem be solved. Perhaps
there would be no need for me to swallow those white pills
after that; no need for them to dissolve and flow in every
vein and artery until they reached my child as the man who
implanted that child knew nothing.

The atmosphere in the apartment helped me to think in
this way. It was an atmosphere which gave me no room for
locking myself in my bedroom. I decided that I would not
swallow those pills. My mother turned the radio up loud
whenever the comedian Ziad Rahbani came on. I enjoyed
listening to his programs. He had a way of drawing laughter
from deep inside you. My mother would sit in the middle
of the apartment, take a needle and start to sew bed-covers,
even as the explosions kept on making the walls shake. We
had grown accustomed to them, unlikely as it may seem, in
the midst of buildings as pock-marked with craters as the
moon's surface.

Tonight I will sleep, and in the morning too, until it is
time for me to go to him . . . But now, as I never did
before, I worry about my best position for sleeping. Shall I
lie on my back? Or on my side? If my mother walks in and
notices my belly, it will ruin all my plans. But that is not the
true reason. The true reason is that I am afraid of harming
the child I carry inside. Was it only in imagination that I felt

a heavy stirring inside me: maybe a couple of movements, maybe three?

How can I guess whether this is the last time I will see the sniper called Sami or whether these steps are being climbed by me one last time? He begins our meeting by saying, "I hope you're feeling better today. I've been really worried about you."

I no more than smile, can add nothing. He comes to me and takes the yellow plastic bag from my hand. Then the words escape from my mouth: "I'm pregnant."

He stands as if nailed to the ground and asks, "How? How can this be? I've been told you could never be pregnant."

"Whoever said that knows nothing about it," I replied.

He shudders and pales, never listening to my reply or trying to realize how my heart pounds and my tongue has gone dry. "What! You mean to say you've used no method of birth control?"

I answer quickly, "I must have made a mistake in taking the pills."

He comes closer. "It's nothing to worry over. I'll send you tomorrow to see an Armenian midwife. She lives near the Mazraa and her name is Azad Wahick. Just tell her that the Regeb family has given you her address." He reaches into his pocket and takes out 100 liras, saying, "Offer her fifty, but if she insists on more, give her the rest."

Looking at the 100-lira note, I can see only its faded blue and grey. Everything else, all other shapes, seem to dissolve. All the world seems to be concentrated in the blue tone of a banknote, as if nothing existed before it or after. It crosses my mind that this blue tint embraces all my thoughts, all the earth, all of space. There is no thought in my head that does not lead to death. Could it ever be possible for me to conceal the way my belly grows bigger and bigger? Could I go on eating and sleeping, yawning and rubbing my eyes as if everything stayed the same?

All my thoughts are channeled into one idea: a quick death from ingesting white pills. But, with aspirin, they will maybe save me by pumping out my stomach. Better to use Demol, which will kill me instantly. I will take it in one quick swallow so that it never even touches my tongue. Why does all this have to happen to me?

People reach a point when they can no longer bear the burden of their bodies, as though disgusted with their bodies' products. To whom should I talk? How am I to find a solution, when every solution the earth offers seems ultimately without meaning? Each thought points towards the one fact: that I have gone through my fourth month of pregnancy. Why did this have to happen to me, not to somebody else? Why didn't I manage to lose myself in the midst of this tumult? Why didn't God lose me Himself? Why does He have to choose me out of thousands of women? Is it that He's forgotten everything I've been through already? Why do these disasters always come in my direction? It's impossible to guess. I feel lost. All I can see is the faded blue of the banknote, which hangs before my eyes as I turn away from where the sniper's feet are rooted to the floor. The background racket has taken on a new sound, a thudding in my ears. I want just to lie down and sleep, to wrap my arms about myself, each arm hugging the opposite shoulder, and draw my knees up to my belly.

Were I to choose to spend whole days and nights searching for the solution, it would not be there to find. Yet here I am, being handed a blue banknote as though the bridge between me and life is open one last time.

Everything seems petty. My thoughts are held back like a butterfly which, as it flutters in a glass cage, knocks its wings against the walls, unbelieving that it can be enclosed in a doorless box when everything around is green, purple and blue. All I want to do is lie in the bathtub and let the warm water flow over me. In its flow I will feel comfort, while its touch will soothe me as if promising relief for my body's swelling. I feel like sitting down. I sit on a step and let my head droop towards my lap. I close my eyes, and the thunder of battle fades in contrast to the sniper's voice, which rattles in my ears. As he shakes me, he yells and shouts. In the midst of his hubbub, I can only think of lying down. "Zahra! What's wrong with you? Have you gone utterly deaf?"

Suddenly it is as if the heat of my feverishness has driven off the water in a cloud of steam, as if a live wire has given me an ice-cold electric shock. I stand up as if ready to explode from the intense heat which my body retains, as if to deny the cool blueness of the banknote. He turns me with my face towards his and says in a stranger's tone, "What's wrong, Zahra? Just tell me why you're angry. Is it because I gave you money? Tell me, please."

I begin to cry exactly as my cousin Ikram did when she was about to be removed to a mental hospital. She wept for no good reason, always in a monotone. The tears which encapsulated her emotions and her madness ran down her cheeks. Her face was like an organic cave, opening and closing its entrance, while a yellow mucus dripped from her nose. I remember the words my mother used: "Her brain is melting."

But unlike Ikram, I now weep with reason. At the sound of the sniper's voice, I want both to stop and to go on crying. Then I begin to say what the doctor has told me.

Holding my face between his hands, the sniper shouts, "He's a liar. Of course a woman can have an abortion after four months."

"Very well, if the doctor's a liar and I'm a liar, then please forget that I spoke. Please forget my swollen belly. It's hardly noticeable. Just let me forget. I want you to forget, as well. I want you to put back in your pocket this blue bit of paper with which you can buy more than a thousand dishes of *foul* and *hummus,* with oil on them, too. And as you sit in the restaurant opposite my window and see only the window aperture staring back at you, and that my family have not enlarged my photograph and hung it there, as usually happens when a young person dies, and so haven't decorated it with black crêpe any more than my mother has placed fresh flowers to replace those that have withered, you will know that this young woman who died has not died according to God's will."

I wish I could die at this very moment and have everything disappear with me. I want to lie with my hands clutching my shoulders, my knees touching my chin. I want to curl up as though I am a foetus again. Did we all come into being unprotesting, in error, often without a woman's cry of pleasure at our moment of conception? There are noises and screams. There is his voice and his shouting. Of one thing I am sure: I don't want to see the blueness of that 100-lira note, I don't want to hear about impossible happenings in the past. I want only to be left alone and in peace, perched at the head of this silent flight of steps.

It feels as if my shoulders and head are being shaken. I lift my face and read his lips as he forms his words: "Very well, Zahra. Please listen to me. Please. Sure we'll get married, but please stop acting like this. I beg you."

Despite the thunder filling my ears, I realize that his

hands have stopped shaking me. No sooner do I look up than I realize that my head was leaning against my knees. I must have been giving rather a strange impression, for he looks at me in intense alarm as he mumbles, his nose projecting sharply and his adam's apple almost jumping out of his throat. He is repeating sentence after sentence: "Please, Zahra. Listen to me. We will get married. Do you hear what I say?"

And I whisper: "I hear you, but my head hurts so much. I want to go home now."

I hear him say quietly: "God damn Satan. Take things easy. Stay here till you're feeling better."

I don't know how much time slips past after that, but I do know I hear him say, "God damn Satan. I'd noticed how your belly was growing, but I told myself it was only because you were eating so much *kibbé* and too much other food."

I don't know how much time slips past, but again I hear him speak: "You know, you really got me frightened. Do you always act like that when you're angry? Is that what happens when you get upset?"

I don't know how much time slips past, but I feel him touch my belly and say, "I hope, God willing, that you will be born to be a fighter, surrounded by the noise of rockets and bazookas."

His comments lift me out of my reverie and drowsiness, but I hear him say nothing more about getting married. I feel as if I am walking intertwined with a cloud that takes me round in circles. As soon as I stand up, he says, "Stay a while. Don't be nervous of your parents. Tomorrow we'll be married. Tell them I am the one you have been with."

As I lie down again on the grubby sheet, my thoughts float free from stagnation. Slowly I form a picture of my

mother, surprised at this birth being so imminent, and hear
her ask what the father does for a living. "Nothing," I will
have to reply. And I see her kiss the ground, thankful that I
have finally given her a son-in-law, especially under such
circumstances.

I feel like sitting up. I sit as the sniper keeps staring at me.

"Tomorrow morning, I'll call at your home and bring my
family."

It leaves me comforted, but also anxious. I don't want my
father to find out I am pregnant, even though his anger can
change nothing. In these times, shouting and screaming and
even sadness have lost their meaning. But I do not wish to
hear my father say, even in mutterings to himself, "Like
mother, like daughter."

All at once, I ask him if he is a sniper. I have only whispered, in case the walls should hear, but he stands up
abruptly, crazy with bitterness, formidable in his anger, and
shouts out, "Sniper? What do you say? You really must be
insane! Do you distrust me to that extent? People now distrust their own mothers, their own fathers! Who has told
you such a thing?"

In my terror I start to quiver. I never dreamed his reaction could be so violent. I cannot believe how the man who
was, a moment before, lying down on the sheet, now stands
over me, threatening my destruction. I go on shaking, but
in self-defense the tremulous words come tumbling out, "I
swear to you, no one knows about my coming here. No
one but you and I, and God who is my witness."

I guard my belly in instinctive protection and continue,
"In the first place, I was hanging washing on the line on my
aunt's roof when I saw you sitting alone with your binoculars and rifle. I thought, then, that you must be a sniper,

from what I'd read in the papers. They'd mentioned there was a sniper about here."

He asks me, "Was this before I saw you there half-naked?"

For some reason I cannot figure out, the question sends another tremor of fear through me. I realize that I'm fully conscious at this moment. My thoughts are clear, my movements no longer paralyzed. He turns his back on me, but I go up to him and say, "I swear by God, and by the present day, to forget everything about it. You're quite right. People begin to distrust even their own shadows. Do you imagine I'd ever have come up here if I'd really thought you were a sniper?"

When he turns back, his face is red and angry. He tries to speak calmly but, instead, bursts out in a scream, "I swear by you and your baby that I'm no sniper! Once I had a shop where I sold clothes in Souk Sursok. It's gone now, and there's no other work. It's for your sake that I come here. Everyone carries a gun these days, from geriatrics to kids in nappies. People need to protect themselves. On the roof that day I was sitting up there to watch the fighting."

As I look at him I smile. My smile disappears in the face of the frown he returns. Catching the remnants of my smile, he pulls me towards him. I lift my hand to protect my belly. I smell his perspiration, feel his prickly beard where it touches my neck. Then he lets me go.

"Do you want to leave now? Tomorrow we'll visit your home, my family and I."

I nod my head, start to say something but change my mind. Then I whisper, "Don't say anything."

Apparently he doesn't understand my meaning because he asks with surprise, "What?"

I repeat what I said before, smiling, "Don't say anything about my belly."

He nods as if he has just awakened and speaks dreamily, "Don't worry. Trust me!"

I say good-bye and run down the stairs as if intending to fly all the way home. I want to tell my mother that I am to be married, but remember, from only last night, how she joined with our neighbor in laughing at me, killing every desire I feel to say anything to her at all. But now, I reason, she will find out for herself when Sami arrives with his family. Sami must be his real name. Otherwise he would have told me today. Can he be a sniper?

I reach the street. It seems as if the war has suddenly come to a stop with his promise that we will marry. Everything seems normal. Has he announced our forthcoming marriage telepathically to all forces to make them stop their shooting and bombardments?

The night is beautiful and I am late. The air is neither hot nor cold, although a few light drops of rain have begun to fall. How wonderful it would be to wake in the morning and hear on the news that the war has finished. Can he be a sniper? I must leave all my anxiety and questioning behind. Once we are married he will, if he is a sniper, ask to be moved to some other duty. Or will he continue to tell me lies whenever he sets out from the house? Where are we to live? In the building where he says (if it is true) that he lives with his family? Or would we do better to rent a house? Why haven't we discussed such details? It's of no importance. We'll speak of them tomorrow. I try to run. I try to skip into the air. My feet don't help me. Why does home seem such a distance? Is it because it is already night? I should cross the street to where the lights from the buildings make the dark less frightening. This is the last time I'll have

to walk along here on my own. I feel afraid. I shouldn't
have stayed out till evening.

In all this relationship I never stayed out so late as I have
tonight. The evening has descended. The street is empty,
except at the barricades. The rain falls. I stumble. I hold on
to a telegraph pole to stop some force from dragging me
down. My thigh hurts. It's hurting even more. I reach down
to touch the place and feel something wet run down my
leg, and on to my foot. Can it be the rain? It's surely not
raining so hard. Am I miscarrying? I can't even walk, but
must not stop. I must reach home. The pain is unbearable. I
can't go on. I fall to the ground. Fear commingles with
pain, strikes into panic. I touch the source of the pain with
my hand and look at what makes it sticky. In spite of the
darkness I can see it is blood. A stray bullet must have
caught me, though I never heard a sound. I heard nothing
except for the pattering of drops of rain. It hurts me each
time the rain touches my face or foot. And a voice rises
from deep inside me and cries, "Help me!" Footsteps and
voices move closer and then recede. Somebody shouts,
"Look out. There's a sniper." And I begin to scream as the
pain leaps up to my neck. "Help me!" My fear makes me
quiver like a decapitated chicken and the whole of my past
and present runs together in my screaming. "Help me!"
The voices remain distant and rain sprinkles my face. I begin to wonder, seeing the buildings despite the darkness. I
stretch my hand out, not knowing in my hallucination
whether these screams are mine or another's.

The pain leaps to my belly and I rake the ground with
my fingers. It was the sniper who put this foetus in my
belly. Is he the one who now puts in all this pain as well? Is
he merely the sniper of the red building? Is he acting deliberately, merely wounding me because he doesn't want to

kill me? Or did he bodge his first shot as I ran across the street? My eyes meet the darkness and the rain falls on my face and soaks me to the skin. The voices fall quiet, except for a whisper now and then. A complete silence descends, for to scream has become an unbearable agony. My vocal cords are chained to my heart's root. The sniper is killing me. His first two bullets missed piercing my head. His third missed piercing the foetus inside me. I don't scream. I don't try to touch the streaming blood. Instead I lie silent in the rain which splatters over the yellow plastic bag that I thought to be my good-luck charm. It is as if I am waiting for each rain-drop to fall. It is as if a distant voice that cries out, "A woman!" seems to echo from the mouth of a far-off cave. It is as if I hear them say, "Don't try to move closer. There's a sniper."

My eyes meet the darkness, and fear, as it grips me, turns to weeping. I wish I could see my mother's face. Where's Ahmad? Where are you, my mother? In what warm room do you sit? I wish I could be close to you now. Why is it that I lie alone in the middle of this street as my blood drains out of me, surrounds me, mixes with the pouring rain?

The pain is terrible, but I grow accustomed to it, and to the darkness. As I close my eyes for an instant, I see the stars of pain. Then there are rainbows arching across white skies. He kills me. He kills me with the bullets that lay at his elbow as he made love to me. He kills me, and the white sheets which covered me a little while ago are still crumpled from my presence. Does he kill me because I'm pregnant? Or is it because I asked him whether he was a sniper? It's as if someone tugs at my limbs. Should I call out one more time, "Please help!"

Although I try, I can hear no sound from my own voice.

The rainbows still arch in the white skies. Rainbow follows rainbow. Sky follows sky. Rainbows of brilliant color pursue each other across skies of blinding whiteness. And though the rain keeps on falling, I do not feel its touch. It's as if a voice says, "Come now, friends." Is it that they intend to try saving me from death? Where's my mother? Is she in one of those warm rooms? I wish I could be with her now, at home. Why am I alone? The darkness becomes fear. My body turns limp and shapeless with fear, as if each muscle and tendon has been severed.

He's killed me. That's why he kept me there till darkness fell. Maybe he couldn't face pulling the trigger and dropping me to the ground in broad daylight. They are trying to drag me away. Someone tugs at my body. The rain touches me again. I still lie where I fell. It's as if someone is saying, "The sniper's still up there," as if they have retreated from me. I close my eyes that perhaps were never truly opened. I see rainbows processing towards me across the white skies with their promises only of menace.

About the Author

HANAN AL-SHAYKH was born in Lebanon in 1945. She was brought up in Beirut before going to Cairo to receive her education. Upon her return to Beirut, she pursued a successful career in journalism, working for the prestigious daily *Al-Nahar* until moving first to the Arabian Gulf, then to London, where she now lives. From a very early stage in her journalistic career, Hanan-al-Shaykh started writing short stories and novels. Her second novel, *Women of Sand and Myrrh*, was first published in the United States in 1992 by Anchor Books.